Magic from the Heart

When Safina did not move, the Chaplain said in a quiet voice:

"Will you stand beside the Bridegroom?"

Words of protest came to her lips, a last plea that she need not be married.

It was then Safina realised that she was in a consecrated place, a Chapel dedicated to God where she could not make an ugly scene.

Slowly, every step forward an agony, Safina moved to stand next to the Duke.

Now that she stood next to him she was aware he was vibrating with anger.

Because the Duke was so tall and overpowering she felt weak and helpless.

She was utterly alone . . .

*A Camfield Novel of Love
by Barbara Cartland*

———

"Barbara Cartland's novels are all distinguished by their intelligence, good sense, and good nature. . . ."
—ROMANTIC TIMES

"Who could give better advice on how to keep your romance going strong than the world's most famous romance novelist, Barbara Cartland?"
—THE STAR

Camfield Place,
Hatfield
Hertfordshire,
England

Dearest Reader,

Camfield Novels of Love mark a very exciting era of my books with Jove. They have already published nearly two hundred of my titles since they became my first publisher in America, and now all my original paperback romances in the future will be published exclusively by them.

As you already know, Camfield Place in Hertfordshire is my home, which originally existed in 1275, but was rebuilt in 1867 by the grandfather of Beatrix Potter.

It was here in this lovely house, with the best view in the county, that she wrote *The Tale of Peter Rabbit*. Mr. McGregor's garden is exactly as she described it. The door in the wall that the fat little rabbit could not squeeze underneath and the goldfish pool where the white cat sat twitching its tail are still there.

I had Camfield Place blessed when I came here in 1950 and was so happy with my husband until he died, and now with my children and grandchildren, that I know the atmosphere is filled with love and we have all been very lucky.

It is easy here to write of love and I know you will enjoy the Camfield Novels of Love. Their plots are definitely exciting and the covers very romantic. They come to you, like all my books, with love.

Bless you,

CAMFIELD NOVELS OF LOVE

by Barbara Cartland

THE POOR GOVERNESS
WINGED VICTORY
LUCKY IN LOVE
LOVE AND THE MARQUIS
A MIRACLE IN MUSIC
LIGHT OF THE GODS
BRIDE TO A BRIGAND
LOVE COMES WEST
A WITCH'S SPELL
SECRETS
THE STORMS OF LOVE
MOONLIGHT ON THE
  SPHINX
WHITE LILAC
REVENGE OF THE HEART
THE ISLAND OF LOVE
THERESA AND A TIGER
LOVE IS HEAVEN
MIRACLE FOR A MADONNA
A VERY UNUSUAL WIFE
THE PERIL AND THE
  PRINCE
ALONE AND AFRAID
TEMPTATION OF A
  TEACHER
ROYAL PUNISHMENT
THE DEVILISH DECEPTION
PARADISE FOUND
LOVE IS A GAMBLE
A VICTORY FOR LOVE
LOOK WITH LOVE
NEVER FORGET LOVE
HELGA IN HIDING
SAFE AT LAST
HAUNTED
CROWNED WITH LOVE
ESCAPE

THE DEVIL DEFEATED
THE SECRET OF THE
  MOSQUE
A DREAM IN SPAIN
THE LOVE TRAP
LISTEN TO LOVE
THE GOLDEN CAGE
LOVE CASTS OUT FEAR
A WORLD OF LOVE
DANCING ON A RAINBOW
LOVE JOINS THE CLANS
AN ANGEL RUNS AWAY
FORCED TO MARRY
BEWILDERED IN BERLIN
WANTED—A WEDDING
  RING
THE EARL ESCAPES
STARLIGHT OVER TUNIS
THE LOVE PUZZLE
LOVE AND KISSES
SAPPHIRES IN SIAM
A CARETAKER OF LOVE
SECRETS OF THE HEART
RIDING IN THE SKY
LOVERS IN LISBON
LOVE IS INVINCIBLE
THE GODDESS OF LOVE
AN ADVENTURE OF LOVE
THE HERB FOR HAPPINESS
ONLY A DREAM
SAVED BY LOVE
LITTLE TONGUES OF FIRE
A CHIEFTAIN FINDS LOVE
THE LOVELY LIAR
THE PERFUME OF THE
  GODS

A KNIGHT IN PARIS
REVENGE IS SWEET
THE PASSIONATE PRINCESS
SOLITA AND THE SPIES
THE PERFECT PEARL
LOVE IS A MAZE
A CIRCUS FOR LOVE
THE TEMPLE OF LOVE
THE BARGAIN BRIDE
THE HAUNTED HEART
REAL LOVE OR FAKE
KISS FROM A STRANGER
A VERY SPECIAL LOVE
THE NECKLACE OF LOVE
A REVOLUTION OF LOVE
THE MARQUIS WINS
LOVE IS THE KEY
LOVE AT FIRST SIGHT
THE TAMING OF A
  TIGRESS
PARADISE IN PENANG
THE EARL RINGS A BELLE
THE QUEEN SAVES THE
  KING
NO DISGUISE FOR LOVE
LOVE LIFTS THE CURSE
BEAUTY OR BRAINS?
TOO PRECIOUS TO LOSE
HIDING
A TANGLED WEB
JUST FATE
A MIRACLE IN MEXICO
WARNED BY A GHOST
TWO HEARTS IN HUNGARY
A THEATER OF LOVE

A NEW CAMFIELD NOVEL OF LOVE BY

BARBARA CARTLAND

Magic From the Heart

JOVE BOOKS, NEW YORK

MAGIC FROM THE HEART

A Jove Book / published by arrangement with
the author

PRINTING HISTORY
Jove edition / February 1992

ISBN: 0-515-10793-X

Jove Books are published by The Berkley Publishing Group,
200 Madison Avenue, New York, New York 10016.
The name "JOVE" and the "J" logo
are trademarks belonging to Jove Publications, Inc.

PRINTED IN THE UNITED STATES OF AMERICA

10 9 8 7 6 5 4 3 2 1

Author's Note

WHEN I came to live in Camfield Place in 1950 I found there was a huge Oak Tree in my garden which had been planted in 1550 by Elizabeth I when she was a prisoner at Hatfield House.

Apparently she rode over from the Marquess of Salisbury's Estate, which borders with mine, and shot her first stag in what is now part of my garden.

Presumably she shot it with a cross-bow and to commemorate her achievement she planted an Oak Tree.

The Oak Tree is still standing and I learnt that locally it had a reputation of bringing people luck.

After I had been at Camfield for some time, I got a friend of mine who was making special items for Ancestral Homes to dip the acorns from the Tree in gold and also the small leaves.

Everyone who has received one from me as a personal present has exclaimed with astonishment at the luck that it has brought them.

I would not like to count how many babies I have produced for people who have despaired of ever having one!

I was told in Scotland that a couple who had been married for fifteen years were longing to have a child, but although the doctor said there was no reason why they should not have one, it never materialised.

I gave the wife vitamins and also one of the Magic Oak Leaves to wear around her neck.

Last Christmas the baby arrived amid great rejoicing and she is now the Champion Baby of the County.

I believe in magic of this sort, and, naturally, my friend who dips the acorns and leaves from the Tree is a White Witch.

When she was a little girl in Canada the Witch who was noted for her help and kindness that she gave to everybody was dying.

She said to this child, "I am going to give you my powers."

My friend who was very young said:

"I do not want your powers."

But the Witch replied:

"You cannot refuse them."

She says now that it is quite extraordinary, but when she does anything for someone she loves and who is a friend, the magic happens and helps other people.

I have always believed that:

"There are more things in Heaven and earth,

Horatio, than are dreamt of in your philosophy!"

When Queen Victoria opened the State Rooms at Hampton Court Palace to the public in 1838, people were horrified.

They said it was impossible to let the "common people" into the grand house, as they would wreck it.

It was not until 1949 that the first Stately House opened its doors to the public for the family's gain.

This was Longleat, the magnificent and beautiful Elizabethan house belonging to the Marquis of Bath.

chapter one

1879

"THE Countess of Sedgewick, Your Grace!"

As the butler announced the visitors, the Duke of Dallwyn, who was writing at his desk, looked up in surprise.

Through the door came a vision in green.

Feathers floated above a lovely face that was dominated by two large, dark eyes.

The Duke rose slowly to his feet.

"Isobel!" he exclaimed.

The door shut behind her and he went on:

"What are you doing here?"

"What do you think?" the Countess answered. "I have come to see you, dearest Crispin."

The Duke moved from behind the desk, and when the Countess held out her hand he ignored it.

1

He walked to stand with his back to the fireplace.

There was silence before he said in an uncompromising tone:

"The last time you spoke to me you told me you hated me and you would never speak to me again!"

"That is what I said," the Countess agreed, "but something has happened, and that is why I am here."

She seated herself elegantly on the sofa, well aware that the light from the window revealed her beauty.

It had been acclaimed by almost every man in London, and the Duke had been one of her most ardent admirers.

As she looked up at him she thought she had almost forgotten how handsome he was.

She could, however, never forget the wild, burning fire which had ignited them both.

The Duke was frowning.

He knew that Isobel Sedgewick would not have come to see him now without some ulterior motive.

He had thought she was a closed chapter in his past, and one which he had no intention of reopening.

"I have something to say to you, Crispin," the Countess said after a little pause, "which I think will be to your advantage."

"If it comes from you, Isobel," the Duke replied, "I am quite certain it will definitely be to my disadvantage, and I have no wish to hear it."

"Now, do not be stupid," the Countess retorted. "I imagine you are still in debt, and that extremely shabby house of yours in the country is falling about your ears."

The Duke made an impatient gesture.

"If it is, it is no business of yours, Isobel."

"That is where you are wrong, and, although I never intended this to happen, my business at the moment is also yours."

The Duke looked at her, and there was an expression of anger in his eyes.

To his surprise, she merely smiled, and after a moment she said:

"You may not believe it, Crispin, after the hard things we said to each other when we parted, but I have always had a soft spot in my heart for you."

"Your heart?" the Duke exclaimed. "I very much doubt if you have one, and personally I have seen no evidence of it."

"Oh, Crispin! Crispin! How can you behave like a petulant small boy instead of what you are, a very alluring man?"

The Duke made an expression of exasperation before he said harshly:

"Let us come to the point. Why are you here?"

"I have a proposition to put to you," the Countess said, "which, as I have already said, will be very much to your advantage."

"I doubt it, but I am prepared to listen," the Duke replied.

The Countess fluttered her eye-lashes and pouted her lips in a manner which most men found irresistible.

The Duke merely stared at her coldly, and after a moment she went on:

"I expect you will remember that Albert has a daughter by his first wife?"

"I had no idea of it," the Duke said briefly, "and if he has, what has it to do with me?"

"Safina is now coming back to England from Florence, where she has been at a Finishing School ever since her father and I were married."

"I will not say the obvious, but it was wise of her to keep away," the Duke remarked with a twist of his lips.

"She had no choice," the Countess answered curtly. "But now that she is over eighteen, they refuse to keep her there any longer."

There was a pause, and as the Duke said nothing, the Countess went on in a different tone of voice:

"You can understand, Crispin, that I have no wish to have a *débutante* hanging round my neck when I am little older than she is, in fact not yet thirty."

The Duke still said nothing.

At the same time, there was just the suspicion of a mocking smile on his lips.

They both knew quite well that Isobel had passed her thirty-third birthday.

"I have no choice but to present Safina at

Court," the Countess went on, "and naturally Albert is planning to give a Ball for her."

"Then she is obviously a very lucky young lady!" the Duke remarked. "Except, of course, she will be over-shadowed by the traditional wicked stepmother!"

"Do you really think I am wicked?" the Countess asked. "You have called me many things, Crispin, things I still remember, but you have never described me as wicked!"

"I would not be surprised at anything you did in order to get your own way!" the Duke answered. "I suppose you are planning to 'dispose' of this wretched girl! Is your choice to be the grave or a Convent?"

"I consider that remark very unkind!" the Countess said as she pouted indignantly. "In fact, I have a far better idea, which is, my dear Crispin, that you should marry her!"

The Duke stared at the Countess as if he could not have heard aright.

Then after what seemed quite a long silence he asked:

"Are you joking?"

"I have never been more serious," the Countess answered.

"Then naturally my answer is 'No' and there is no need for us to go on talking about it," the Duke replied. "So I think, Isobel, you should now leave, for we really have nothing more to say to each other."

He put out his hand towards the bell-pull.

Before he could reach it, the Countess said:

"Wait! I have not finished!"

"There is nothing more to say," the Duke retorted. "I cannot imagine how you thought up anything so utterly ridiculous as that I should marry your Stepdaughter!"

He drew in his breath before he continued:

"If you want the truth, I think it is just an excuse to come here to taunt me!"

"You are reacting exactly as I expected you would," the Countess said disarmingly. "But as I have often said before, you look very handsome, Crispin, when you are angry!"

She gave a soft, seductive little laugh before she added:

"I remember how angry you were when you found Edward kissing me? And how exciting it was when I said I was sorry, and you forgave me?"

Her words seemed almost to float on the air.

When the Duke did not speak, she went on:

"You could be very brutal when you were jealous! But you have to admit it excited both of us!"

"Stop!"

The Duke almost shouted the word.

"What are you trying to do, Isobel? Why are you raking up the past? When we parted, I told you I loathed and despised you for the way you had treated me."

He paused a moment and then went on:

"I was foolish enough to believe that although

you were unfaithful to your husband, you would be faithful to me!"

He blurted out the words as if he were unable to control them.

Then he said:

"For God's sake—go! You disillusioned me once, and I have no wish to even think of you again!"

"But sometimes you cannot help it," the Countess said softly, "and although you will not believe me, it is the same with me."

"But of course you have plenty of other men to console you," the Duke retorted. "When they talk about you at Whites Club, I find myself thinking there is not a man in the room who has not been your lover at some time or another."

"It is an enjoyable idea, but it is not quite true," the Countess said. "Be sensible enough to understand, Crispin, that is why I have no intention of sitting on a dais amongst the Dowagers—not, at least, for another ten years!"

"If you are going to suggest again that I marry your Stepdaughter," the Duke said, "you can save your breath. So goodbye, Isobel. As I said before, I hope I never see you again—at any rate, alone."

Once again he put out his hand towards the bell-pull, but the Countess said quickly:

"Wait! I have two more things to say which will convince you that you are making a mistake."

The Duke's hand halted.

At the same time, he squared his chin, and there was a hard, obstinate expression on his face which those who knew him were aware was ominous.

"The first reason why you should marry Safina is quite simple," the Countess said. "She comes into some money when she marries—about thirty thousand pounds. The great bulk of her mother's fortune will be mine and mine alone for as long as Albert is alive."

"I am not interested!" the Duke said coldly.

"Then you should be!" the Countess replied. "Thirty thousand pounds should pay off most of your debts, and the prospect for the future is fantastic."

"I have told you I am not interested," the Duke said, "and as for waiting until Albert is dead, I am quite certain that, Witch that you are, he will live for eternity."

He spoke with a bitterness in his voice that was unmistakable, but the Countess merely laughed.

"So now I am a Witch!" she said. "You always said I bewitched you, but then, if I remember rightly, I was a goddess and you worshipped at my feet!"

"I was a fool!" the Duke said.

"A very ardent, demanding, authoritative fool!" the Countess murmured.

"The answer to your proposition is still 'No'!" the Duke said.

"You have only heard the first reason why you

should accept it," the Countess replied.

"And what is the second?" the Duke asked.

"I have two letters," the Countess answered, "which I took yesterday from the *secrétaire* in Yvonne de Mauzon's Boudoir."

The Duke stiffened.

"Two letters?" he asked, incredulous.

"They were charmingly expressed and, of course, some of the phrases were familiar."

"What are you saying, and why did you take these letters?" the Duke asked angrily.

"I thought, dear Crispin, if you were a reluctant Bridegroom, as you appear to be, they would be of considerable interest to the Ambassador."

There was a silence in the Study in which it would have been possible to hear a pin drop.

The Duke seemed turned to stone, and the Countess, watching him, did not move.

The Duke broke the silence.

"You would not dare!"

"I am not exaggerating when I say that I would do anything rather than have Albert's tiresome brat on my hands."

The Duke walked across the room and stood at the window to look out with unseeing eyes.

He knew that Isobel, when she wished to get her own way, would stop at nothing.

She also wanted to punish him for having left her.

He had discovered once that when he was away, she had taken to her bed not one, but two of his friends.

He had believed, foolishly, that she loved him as much as she was capable of loving anyone.

It had disgusted him that she could not be faithful for the few days in which he had left London because his mother was ill.

They had quarrelled violently.

He had stormed out of the house saying he would never speak to her again.

He had loathed her because she had destroyed his love.

It had all happened a year before.

He was well aware of the procession of men who had followed him.

He himself had found consolation with the attractive, seductive wife of the French Ambassador.

The Frenchman was, however, very different from the ageing Earl of Sedgewick.

If the Earl had any suspicion of what was going on behind his back, he did not want to know about it.

He was busy with his position at Court, his duties as Lord Lieutenant of his County, and the administration of his very large possessions.

The Duke was aware, as was everybody else, that his first wife had been extremely rich.

Her fortune had increased as her relatives died and she inherited their wealth.

Vaguely the Duke remembered hearing that because she had adored her husband, she had left him her enormous fortune to do with as he pleased.

It was not surprising that Isobel, with her scheming mind, was determined to acquire every penny she could before she became a widow.

Only on the Earl's death would it go to any children of his two marriages.

The Duke suspected that Isobel had no intention, because it might spoil her beauty, of producing a child, not even the heir for whom the Earl obviously had married someone very much younger than himself.

He needed money, the Duke thought. God knew that was true.

But he had no intention of selling his title to obtain it, or of marrying Isobel's stepdaughter because she wished to be rid of her.

But that she intended to blackmail him with letters he had written to Yvonne de Mauzon made the situation quite different.

It was known to every man in London that the Ambassador was exceedingly jealous.

This was understandable considering his wife was not only beautiful, but had an indescribable fascination.

She had only to smile at a man and look at him from under her eye-lashes for him to feel the blood throbbing in his temples.

The Duke in all his many love-affairs had never known a woman so insatiable or so provocative.

From the moment Yvonne de Mauzon smiled at him with an invitation in her eyes, he had been intrigued, then captivated to the point where he knew he would never rest until he had become her lover.

They had to be very circumspect, but fortunately the Ambassador was frequently obliged to return to France.

When he and Yvonne met, he found the stories about her were not exaggerated.

The Duke was only waiting impatiently now for her to tell him when it would be safe for them to meet again.

Set beside her, no other woman seemed interesting, let alone desirable.

He knew, however, he was now caught in a trap.

Isobel was closing the door by which there was any chance of escape.

For the moment, to save himself from destruction, he turned from the window to say:

"I cannot believe Yvonne would be so foolish as to keep any letter I wrote to her. You have always been a liar, Isobel, but if, as you claim, they really exist, I wish to see them."

The Countess laughed.

"That is just what I expected you to say, and I therefore came prepared."

"You have them with you?"

It flashed through the Duke's mind that in that case he could take the letters from her and burn them in the fire.

What had dissolved to ashes could certainly not be held against him.

However plausibly Isobel might describe what

had once been in her possession, who would listen?

She was opening her reticule, which was the same green as her gown.

She drew out some sheets of paper which she held out invitingly to the Duke.

He took them from her.

As soon as he looked at what was in his hand, he said:

"These are copies!"

"Of course, dear Crispin! Would I be so foolish as to trust you with the originals when there is a fire burning in the room, and you are so much stronger than I am?"

The Duke glanced again at the papers he held in his hand.

Then he threw them into the fire and watched as they turned to ashes.

"I can make you other copies if you want," Isobel offered.

She was taunting him, and he felt like striking her.

He had beaten her once when he was so wildly jealous that he could not control himself.

He knew she had enjoyed it, just as she was now enjoying torturing him.

With a superhuman effort he said in a conciliatory tone of voice:

"Shall we talk this over sensibly?"

"There is nothing sensible about my having to chaperon Albert's daughter!" Isobel said in a hard voice. "You will marry her, Crispin, because there is nothing else you can do."

The Duke wanted to rage at her, but he would not lower himself.

"Pass her on to somebody else," he suggested, "who is more in need of money than I am!"

"If he is a Duke, I can see no particular difficulty," Isobel replied.

The Duke did his best to think of a Duke who was in the same position as himself, and failed.

Northumberland, Newcastle, Roxburghe, Sutherland, Norfolk—all of them were rich.

There was no reason for any of them to have to sell their titles.

For a moment he thought of telling Isobel to do her worst.

After all, the Duke of Wellington had told Harriette Wilson to "publish and be damned."

She had tried to blackmail him by saying she would write about him in her memoirs.

Then he knew he would not only have to fight a duel with the Ambassador, but also would be sacrificing Yvonne.

It was something no gentleman could do to a woman who had trusted him with her reputation.

He was well aware that Yvonne was terrified of her husband.

She was telling the truth when she had said he might kill her if he ever had any reason to suspect her of being unfaithful.

No, he was caught, and the door of the trap was closed.

Isobel's long, thin fingers had turned the key securely in the lock.

In a voice that did not sound like his own, he said with an effort:

"What do you want me to do?"

"I thought you would see sense," Isobel said, "and I will tell you exactly."

She settled herself more comfortably on the sofa.

The Duke stood in front of the fire, feeling that his whole body was cold and he had turned to stone.

"Safina is arriving from Florence in three days time," Isobel began. "I will meet her not in London, but at Dover, and I will bring her to Wyn, where you will be married in your Private Chapel."

The Duke clenched his hands so that the knuckles turned white, but he did not speak.

"You will then go off on your honeymoon, and no one will see Safina or even know she exists," she went on, "until Albert, having recovered from the shock, announces it in the *Gazette*."

"What is he going to think?" the Duke asked.

"I shall tell him that you met Safina when you were in Florence and fell madly in love with her. However, afraid she might be carried off by some other suitor, you married her while you had the chance!"

"And you really believe your husband will swallow all that nonsense?" the Duke asked.

"Albert leaves for Edinburgh tomorrow morning, on a special mission for the Queen. He is going with a friend in his yacht, therefore will be out of touch with everything that is occurring here for nearly three weeks."

The Countess gave a little sigh.

"It is what would have delighted you, Crispin, when we meant so much to each other."

The Duke ignored the last remark and said:

"Do you really think your husband will accept a marriage which took place without his permission and which therefore will be, I think, illegal?"

Isobel laughed.

"You will not get out of it that way, Crispin! What father would not be delighted that his daughter had married a Duke?"

"Suppose the girl objects—which she should do."

"You can leave Safina to me."

"Then I can only say I am extremely sorry for the girl!" the Duke remarked sarcastically.

"You can, of course, dear Crispin, make it up to her in your own inimitable way!"

There was silence. Then the Duke said:

"Do not do this to me, Isobel. If you have only memory of the happiness we once shared, you will find another man, and I am sure there are many, who will take this girl off your hands."

He realised as he spoke that he was pleading with the Countess.

At the same time, he was desperate.

He was losing everything—his freedom, his hope that one day he would have a happy marriage.

Also, he told himself savagely, his self-respect.

He knew as he finished speaking that it was a waste of time to make any sort of appeal to Isobel.

She had always been as hard as nails.

It was only her exotic sensuality that had made her warm and clinging in bed.

She could be cruel, indifferent, and extremely vindictive.

Now she laughed and answered:

"I remember all that and a great deal more, and I also remember how you raged at me, how you left me. Then, judging from your letters, Yvonne has managed to console you for any discomfort you might have been suffering!"

It was clear from the way she spoke that she was jealous that he had been comforted in the arms of Yvonne.

He had found in her what he had found in Isobel—a lovely, sensuous woman.

She could light a fire which while they were making love would consume them both.

It would be wildly, exhilaratingly exciting.

But the fires of passion could also burn themselves out.

Isobel knew that was what had happened to him where she was concerned.

Because she was a woman, she was jealous, she wanted to torture him, to make him suffer, and make him subservient to her.

He realised there was nothing more he could say.

Some pride that was very much a part of his character made him accept the inevitable without belittling himself any further.

"Very well, Isobel," he said at last, "I will accept this intolerable situation on one condition—that you give me back the letters you stole from Yvonne."

He paused a moment and then went on:

"I do not trust you, and I swear I will not put the ring on your stepdaughter's finger until the letters are safely in my hands."

It took the Countess a moment to find a solution to this.

Finally she said:

"Very well, Crispin. I will bring them with me to Wyn, and give them to you in the Chapel once the Marriage Ceremony has begun."

"I shall, of course, examine them to make sure they are genuine," the Duke warned her.

"And if they are not—what then?"

"You can take the girl away with you."

"You will receive your letters," Isobel promised.

She rose to her feet and once again the Duke reached out towards the bell-pull, but she was in his way.

"We have made a bargain together," she said softly, "and I think you should seal it with a kiss, just for old time's sake."

"I would rather kiss a serpent of Satan!" the Duke retorted. "I hated you, Isobel, for what you did to me when I loved you, and now I despise you as well as I despise myself for ever becoming involved with you!"

He realised as he spoke that this outburst was not what she expected.

He knew full well how conceited she was, and with reason.

There had never been a man she had not been able to twist round her little finger, and manipulate in any way she wished.

He saw the surprise in her eyes.

He thought that behind the façade of a sophisticated woman there were still the remnants of the young girl who wanted to conquer the Social World, and had succeeded.

In a slightly calmer voice he said:

"You have forced me into doing against my will something you wish me to do. Be content, and I can only beg you to leave me alone in the future."

As he spoke he deliberately reached behind her and rang the bell.

As he did so, he became vividly conscious of the exotic perfume she always used.

How well he remembered its seductive scent which clung to him long after he had left her.

As the door opened and the Butler appeared, he said:

"Goodbye, Countess. It was very kind of you to call on me, and of course I shall be waiting to hear further details of what we have been discussing."

Isobel put out her hand, and he raised it perfunctorily to his lips.

Then, as she moved across the room to where the Butler was waiting, he walked to the window.

He could not bear to look at her any longer.

He heard the door shut.

Then his self-control broke.

He no longer had to force himself to behave with propriety.

He was cursing beneath his breath, damning Isobel into the Hell which he knew was waiting for him.

A Hell in which he would be imprisoned for the rest of his life.

chapter two

"I SHALL miss you, Reverend Mother, and thank you for all the kindness you have shown me since I have been here."

Safina spoke with an unmistakable note of sincerity in her voice.

The Mother Superior smiled.

"It has been a pleasure having you, Safina," she said, "and I hope when you go out into the world, you will remember what we have taught you."

"I shall remember all of it," Safina declared, "and to be honest, Reverend Mother, I wish I did not have to leave you."

The Mother Superior put her hand on Safina's shoulder.

"You are now grown up and you have a position in life to fulfil. Do not forget there are people who will try to follow your example and those you will inspire. You must not fail them."

"I will try not to," Safina promised.

"God go with you, my child," the Mother Superior said.

Safina curtsied, kissed the Mother Superior's hand, and walked towards the door.

As she left, the Mother Superior looked after her with a look of affection and also of anxiety.

She had not liked the letter she had received from the Countess of Sedgewick.

It contained instructions about the journey Safina was to take to England.

It seemed to the Mother Superior that it was hard and unfeeling.

She had the idea that when she returned home, Safina would miss her own mother even more than she had done when she first came to the Convent School.

Then, she had been desperately unhappy.

It was only because the Nuns had been understanding, and the other pupils nice, well-born girls, that she had gradually acclimatized herself.

Then, as she had said, she enjoyed being at School.

As Safina drove away through the streets of Florence, she was saying goodbye.

She thought that no place in the world, even

England, could be so beautiful or so redolent with history.

The Mother Superior had sent with her, on her stepmother's instructions, a Nun to take her safely to her own country.

Sister Benedict was an elderly woman and an extremely intelligent one.

She had been born into an Aristocratic Italian Family.

She had taken her vows only when the man to whom she was engaged was killed in a duel.

Although it had been an arranged marriage, as was usual amongst the aristocratic Families of Europe, she had loved him.

She therefore felt she could not face the world without him, and entered the Convent.

The School was a separate part of it and she had not intended to be involved with the young girls.

But she had been very well educated herself.

She was also so intelligent that she had finally been persuaded by the Mother Superior to teach as well as to pray.

Now, as they passed over over the Ponte Vecchio, which spanned the river, Safina said impulsively:

"I shall miss all this, Sister, it is so beautiful."

"Wherever you go, it will remain in your heart," Sister Benedict replied, "but I know when you get to England you will find that beautiful too."

"It is beautiful," Safina answered, "and I am

looking forward to being in my father's house in the country."

She paused for a moment before she went on:

"I am thinking of the horses I can ride, of the beauty of the woods, and the gardens which my mother loved."

She was thinking as she spoke how painful it would be to walk in the Rose Garden and over the smooth green lawns without her mother.

When she was a very small child, her mother had taken her every day into the garden.

She had told her stories about the flowers, the herbs, the birds, and the butterflies.

The garden had become part of Safina's dreams.

She had not only dreamt of it, but it had been in her imagination all the years she had been away in Florence.

She had felt when she was alone at night that she could walk in the garden at home.

She could smell the scent of the flowers and hear the song of the birds.

"I will soon do that in reality," she told herself now, "but it will not be the same without Mama."

It was then inevitably that she remembered her Stepmother.

She had known since the day her father had married again that his new wife disliked her.

She not only saw it in her eyes, but heard it in

the hard voice she used when she spoke to her.

When she first learnt that her father was to marry someone very much younger than himself, she thought perhaps it would be rather fun.

If her Stepmother was young, they could laugh together.

It might even alleviate some of the misery she felt at losing her mother.

She was quickly disillusioned.

Isobel had made it absolutely clear the moment she and the Earl of Sedgewick were married that Safina was to go away.

"Safina is old enough for Finishing School, dearest Albert," she said in the soft, cooing voice which meant she wanted something.

She smiled beguilingly at her husband and went on:

"As she is so pretty, it would be a great mistake for her to be ignorant and badly educated like so many young girls."

"Of course." Safina remembered her father had agreed.

He was obviously besotted with his new wife.

Safina resented it because she thought it insulted the memory of her mother, yet she was intelligent enough to understand.

He had been at first stricken by the death of his wife and had seemed to grow old in just a few weeks.

He mooned about dismally and found it hard to attend even to his duties at Court.

It was then, quite unexpectedly, that Safina noticed a glint in his eye and a different note in his voice.

She had not understood why until she heard from one of her relations what was happening.

"There is no fool like an old fool," her aunt had said tartly, "and that applies to your father!"

Safina stared at her, not understanding until she explained:

"You are going to have a Stepmother, and I think it is my duty to tell you so before you hear the news from your father and upset him by making a scene."

"I will . . . not do . . . that," Safina said.

At the same time, she felt like crying because her father had forgotten her mother so soon.

As if her aunt knew what she was thinking, she said:

"You know as well as I do, Safina, that your father needs an heir. Sedgewick is an Ancient Earldom of which we are all proud."

Safina had not thought of it before.

Now she remembered her father's Heir Presumptive was a nephew whom none of them had ever liked.

He had been sent out to Australia because he was so extravagant.

Her father had paid his debts a dozen times and had refused to support him any longer.

She could understand that all her relations had wanted her father and mother to have a son.

Any failure was no fault of their own.

As her mother had said:

"It is not God's will."

Safina was therefore an only child.

Bravely she said to her aunt:

"Of course I hope Papa will have a son, and it will be very exciting for me to have a brother."

"You are a sensible girl," her aunt said approvingly.

Safina had therefore forced herself to welcome Isobel.

Yet she knew at their first meeting that there was no longer a welcome for her in her own home.

Her father was very happy.

She had therefore tried to tell herself all the way to Florence that it would be very selfish to wish him to be anything else.

She only knew that it was agonising to see Isobel in her mother's place.

It hurt her to see her wearing the Sedgewick Jewels and re-arranging the rooms.

It was with the greatest difficulty that Safina prevented herself from saying that it was her mother's money which had made everything so luxurious at Wick Park.

It was her mother's money which allowed Isobel to spend a fortune on clothes, furs, and anything else she fancied.

"I must try to love her for Papa's sake," Safina instructed herself.

But she knew that every hour she spent with Isobel made her dislike her more than she did already.

It was therefore in a way a relief to be sent away to Florence.

Isobel had in addition persuaded her father that it would be a mistake for Safina to come home for holidays.

"It is such a long way, dearest Albert," she said, "and very unsettling for a young girl. She will have friends amongst the other pupils, and I am sure they will take her out occasionally. It is what happened to me when I was at School."

The Earl agreed, as he always did, to anything his new wife suggested.

So Safina, in her own words, went into exile.

It might be three years before she would see England or her home again.

"If you cannot come to me, my darling child," her father said, "I promise I will come to you."

Somehow Isobel prevented that.

She wanted to go to Europe, but the El Dorado of every beautiful woman was Paris.

Safina learnt, not from her father, where they were.

Some of the other pupils had heard from their parents that Isobel had conquered the French with her beauty.

She had given a large Ball in the house in the Champs-Élysées, which she had persuaded the Earl to rent for a month.

"Of course, her gowns," one of the girls told Safina, "are from the smartest dressmakers, and her jewels are envied by every woman who sees them."

Her father's letters—he wrote to her dutifully every week—said very little about the visit to Paris.

He had some important meetings, he said, with the Prime Minister and a most interesting one with the Emperor.

The Earl was not a particularly gifted writer, but Safina loved his letters.

They were the only thing that linked her with England and the past.

Because she was intelligent, she applied herself to learning, not only to everything the Nuns could teach her, but to the extra lessons she had from a number of Special Tutors.

They taught subjects beyond the ordinary curriculum of the School.

She was therefore now proficient not only in French and Italian, but also in German and Spanish.

She had lessons in many other subjects also, especially this last year, when she was older than all the other pupils.

It had been quite unnecessary for her to attend the ordinary classes.

What the girls were learning she had learnt the previous year.

The journey across France was tiring yet interesting.

When they reached Calais their Courier, who had escorted them from Florence, said:

"There's a boat leaving in an hour's time, M'Lady, and I've engaged a cabin for you and the Sister."

"Thank you," Safina replied, "but I hope I shall not feel sea-sick. After being shut up in the train for so long, I am looking forward to the sea-air."

Sister Benedict, however, was a bad sailor and immediately lay down in the cabin.

Safina walked around the deck, escorted by the Courier.

He was a middle-aged Italian who had travelled to many parts of the world.

She found what he told her interesting.

But she was feeling very excited at the thought of seeing her own country again.

"However difficult Stepmama may be," she told herself, "I shall feel Mama is with me, and when I walk in the gardens or ride in the woods, I shall think of no-one but her."

When they arrived at Dover there was an English Courier waiting to meet her.

To her surprise, he informed her that she was not to go to London.

She had expected to find her father waiting for her there.

Then, after staying one night at Sedgewick House in Park Lane, they would go to Wick Hall.

It was Friday, and she knew he always liked

to spend the weekend at Wick.

"Where am I going?" she asked the Courier.

"I was told, Lady Safina," he replied, "just to inform you that Her Ladyship'll meet you at the place to where I'm taking you, and I'm to answer no questions until we get there."

He spoke in a somewhat embarrassed manner, and Safina looked at him in astonishment.

She could not understand why her Stepmother should be so mysterious.

"Where is my father?" she asked.

The Courier hesitated.

For one terrifying moment Safina wondered if her father was ill or dead.

Finally, as if he felt compelled to answer, the Courier said:

"His Lordship's on his way to Edinburgh."

"To Edinburgh!" Safina exclaimed. "Why is Papa going there?"

It seemed to her very strange that her father should go away just as she was returning home.

In his last letter he had said:

I am not quite certain when your Step-mother is planning for you to arrive in England, but I assure you, my dear, I am waiting eagerly to see you and we will have so much to talk about.

"I think," the Courier was saying, "that His Lordship had to go on a Special Mission for Her Majesty."

He paused before continuing:

"I know the Duke of Hamilton'll be his host while he's in Edinburgh."

"Papa has not written me a letter?" Safina enquired.

"I'm sure Her Ladyship'll have one for you," the Courier replied.

He was an elderly man who Safina remembered had looked after them in the past.

She had a feeling he was upset by something and was, in fact, not being completely frank with her.

Why she should think that, she had no idea.

It was just something she felt, and what she thought of as her perception was seldom wrong.

"Her Ladyship sent a maid who's waiting now at the Hotel," the Courier continued, "and I thought, M'Lady, you'd like something to eat and drink before we set off for the place where you're to stay the night."

It all seemed very strange to Safina.

However, it seemed better not to go on asking questions while Sister Benedict and the Italian Courier were listening.

They were to return to Florence immediately.

She said goodbye to them, thanking them both for looking after her.

She tipped the Courier generously, having put the money into an envelope.

She had a present for Sister Benedict which she knew would delight her when she opened it.

She kissed the Nun goodbye, saying:

"Thank you ... thank you ... for being so kind, and please do not forget me."

"You know I will remember you in my prayers," Sister Benedict replied, "and may God and His Angels guard you."

Safina felt the tears come into her eyes.

She turned away and stepped into the carriage which the English Courier, Mr. Carter, had waiting for her.

They drove to the Hotel.

She found he had ordered her a light meal just in case she had been sea-sick on the voyage.

She was not hungry, but she ate what had been provided and then was ready to continue the journey.

The maid who was to travel with her was a servant she had never seen before.

She seemed, for no reason Safina could ascertain, somewhat hostile.

She had expected they would be driving to the Railway Station, so she was surprised when she learnt just before they left that they were going across country.

There was no train service, and they had to travel by road.

"I cannot understand," she said as she stepped into the carriage, "why we are not going to Wick Park."

"Her Ladyship'll explain everything," Mr. Carter said quickly.

He climbed up onto the box with the Coachman.

As they drove out of Dover, Safina asked the maid, whose name she had learnt was Smith, if she had any idea where they were going.

" 'Er Ladyship just sends me down t'Dover with Mr. Carter," the maid answered, " 'nd I were told nothin'."

She sounded cross about it, and Safina said:

"It all seems a very mysterious idea. I did hope I was going to Wick."

"I were there a week ago wit' 'Is Lordship," the maid said.

"Was it looking beautiful?" Safina enquired.

"Th' flowers were a-comin' out."

"My mother used to think that nothing was lovelier than Wick in the Spring," Safina said. "She often used to quote Robert Browning saying: 'Oh to be in England now that April's there.' "

Smith made no reply, and Safina thought there was no point in going on talking to her.

Instead, she imagined herself back at Wick and seeing the almond blossoms in bloom.

The daffodils would be a golden carpet under the Oak Trees in the Park.

"I must go there soon, very soon," she told herself.

It was a long journey and a tiring one.

The road in some places was narrow and twisting so that the four horses that drew the carriage had to go slowly.

It was growing dark when finally they turned into the courtyard of a Posting House.

It was quite obvious that that was what it was, and again Safina was surprised.

Her father always avoided staying at Inns or Posting Houses.

Invariably, if they went anywhere, he arranged that they should stay with one of his many friends.

She was quite certain that there would be people he knew in this part of England.

It therefore seemed extraordinary that her Stepmother should be waiting for her at what was an ordinary Posting House.

It had nothing, as far as she could see, to recommend it.

It certainly was not popular, for there were no other carriages in the courtyard, nor did there seem to be many Stables on the other side of it.

The Inn-Keeper, a fat, burly man, was waiting at the doorway and bowed to her respectfully.

"Yer Ladyship be expected," he said to Safina.

He went ahead before she could answer him down a narrow passage.

They passed what she saw was a Dining-Room with just three people having dinner.

At the end of the passage there was an Oak door.

The Inn-Keeper opened it.

Safina realised that it was a Private Parlour.

There was a fire burning at the end of the room, and seated in front of it was her Stepmother.

One glance told Safina that Isobel was as beautiful as she had been when she left England.

But she was more elegantly dressed and heavily bejewelled.

"You are late," Isobel said as Safina walked towards her. "I began to wonder what had happened to you."

"It was a long way," Safina answered, "and the roads were narrow and not like the main Highways."

"Well, anyway, you are here," Isobel said. "I expect you wish to tidy yourself before Dinner."

"Thank you, I would like that," Safina said.

Isobel turned towards the Inn-Keeper, who was hovering in the doorway.

"Take Her Ladyship upstairs and see that my maid attends to her," she ordered.

"Very good, M'Lady."

Safina followed him back down the passage and up an ancient wooden staircase.

She thought it was a strange way to be greeted after being away from England for three years.

'She still hates me,' she thought with a little sigh.

It was obvious that the years since they had met had not mitigated Isobel's dislike for her.

She tidied herself in a quite pleasant room.

Isobel's maid was a nervous creature who had

obviously been told not to talk to Safina.

She arranged Safina's hair and poured some warm water into a basin so that Safina could wash.

Safina then hurried downstairs to find a table had now been laid in the Private Parlour.

Isobel, as she had expected, was waiting impatiently.

"Come along," she said, "there is no-one here for you to titivate yourself for, and we have to leave early in the morning, so I want to get to bed."

"Where are we going?" Safina asked.

"I will tell you that later," Isobel replied.

The food was brought in.

It was so much better than she expected that Safina guessed Isobel had brought most of it with her.

She was also given a glass of wine that had come from her father's cellar.

"Did Papa give you a letter for me?" she asked as she sipped it. "I am so disappointed to hear that he has gone to Scotland."

"Who told you that?" Isobel snapped.

"Mr. Carter, when I asked him."

There was silence, and then Isobel said:

"Yes, he has gone to Scotland."

"I am sure he was disappointed not to be able to meet me."

"He did not think you were arriving for another fortnight," Isobel remarked.

Safina stared at her.

"Are you saying Papa does not know I am in England?"

"There was no point in my telling him you were coming, when he could do nothing about it."

"But *you* wrote to the Mother Superior telling her to send me home at once. I was rather surprised that it was not Papa."

"I wrote because I wished you to arrive now," Isobel replied in an uncompromising tone.

Safina felt even more bewildered.

There was, however, no point in saying so when the maids kept coming in and out with the food.

When they finished, the table was moved away.

Then, as they walked back to the fire, Safina said:

"Do tell me, Stepmama, what all this mystery is about. Why have we come here and where are we going?"

Isobel hesitated, then she said:

"I am tired. I will tell you everything tomorrow. As it is, I can hardly keep my eyes open."

She walked across the room as she spoke, opened the door, and walked away down the passage.

Safina stared after her.

She could not understand what was happening.

And despite trying to be sensible, she was frightened.

Her father did not know she was in England and Isobel would not say that they were here or where they were going.

There was nothing she could do except go up to bed.

Smith was waiting for her and was obviously in a disagreeable mood.

Safina therefore undressed in silence.

When she was alone and in bed, she went over in her mind the extraordinary events of the day.

She now felt even more frightened.

Where was Isobel taking her? Why was she so mysterious about it?

Was she to be locked away in another School?

That seemed impossible, because she was too old.

But why was there all this secrecy?

Why for the first time in her life was she staying in a Posting House and not with one of her father's friends?

Although she was agitated, she was tired after the long train journey and fell asleep.

She was woken by Smith rattling back the curtains.

Then she poured some hot water into the basin on the Washhandstand and said:

"You'd better get up, M'Lady. We're leaving in 'alf an hour."

"Where to?" Safina asked.

Smith did not answer, and Safina knew it was no use trying to make her.

She dressed herself quickly.

When she went downstairs to breakfast, she found she was having it alone.

Isobel obviously had hers brought up to her bedroom.

At any other time Safina would have thought this was to be expected.

But she now had the uncomfortable feeling that Isobel did not intend to talk to her until they were in the carriage.

As she finished her breakfast, the Inn-Keeper opened the Parlour door to say:

"Oi be told to tell ye 'Er Ladyship's waitin' an' in a 'urry."

Safina jumped to her feet.

She put her travelling-cloak over her shoulders and picked up her hand bag.

The Inn-Keeper went ahead of her, down the passage and into the court-yard.

Outside, she saw the carriage waiting.

Then she realised there was another carriage behind it in which there was the Courier and the two Lady's-Maids.

As Safina joined Isobel, she saw that her Stepmother was very smartly dressed.

Her hat fluttered with crimson feathers, her dress was of the same colour, her cloak was trimmed with sable.

There were diamonds around her neck and in her ears.

When she moved her hand, there was a glitter of the bracelets on her wrist.

The footman placed a rug over their knees and

the four horses were driven out of the court-yard.

They were a different team from the one which had drawn Safina yesterday.

She waited for Isobel to speak, but when she said nothing, she said politely:

"Good morning, Stepmama. I hope you slept well."

"It was hardly likely in a place like that," Isobel replied scornfully.

"I thought it strange that we did not stay, as we always used to do, with one of Papa's friends."

She paused before continuing:

"I am not quite certain where we are, but he knows a great number of people in the South of England."

Isobel did not reply for a moment, and then she said:

"If you are interested in where you are, we are on our way to Wyn Park."

"Wyn Park?" Safina declared in a puzzled tone. "Why are we going there?"

"For you to be married," Isobel replied.

Safina felt she must have misunderstood her.

"What did . . . you say?" she asked.

"I told you," Isobel said in a little louder voice, "that we are going to Wyn Park, where you will marry the Duke of Dallwyn."

Safina stared at her.

"I do not . . . understand what . . . you are . . . saying!" she exclaimed.

"I should have thought it was quite clear to anyone who is not a half-wit," Isobel replied. "I have arranged for you to marry the Duke of Dallwyn, and you are an extremely fortunate young woman."

Safina drew in her breath.

"I am . . . sorry, Stepmama," she said, "to contradict . . . you but I have no . . . intention of . . . marrying the Duke of Dallwyn or . . . anyone else!"

"You will do as you are told," Isobel said. "Everything is arranged, and there is no use making a scene, for there is nothing you can do about it."

"Of course . . . there is . . . something I can . . . do about it," Safina declared.

She paused before continuing:

"I can . . . refuse to marry . . . the Duke, and I am . . . sure Papa will . . . support me. He will agree that I am . . . not to be . . . forced into some hole-and-corner . . . marriage with . . . a stranger!"

She spoke bravely, but at the same time she was feeling frightened.

She was alone with Isobel, and no-one else knew where she was.

"I thought that would be your attitude," Isobel replied, "but let me tell you, it is a very stupid one."

Safina did not speak, and after a few seconds Isobel said:

"As you doubtless know, in Italy, where you

have just come from, marriages are always arranged, as they are in France and England amongst the aristocrats. You should therefore be extremely grateful that I have chosen a Duke to be your husband."

"*You* have chosen," Safina objected. "That is what is ... wrong. Why has Papa not ... told me who he ... wants me to marry? And ... of course I cannot be ... married in his ... absence."

"You will be married as soon as we arrive," Isobel said, "and if you scream and make a fuss, I shall tell the servants to hold you down while the ring is put on your finger!"

Safina stared at her.

She knew by the sharp tone of Isobel's voice that she was determined to have her own way.

However, she would not be intimidated.

"How dare you suggest anything so ... disgraceful and ... wrong when it concerns the Sacrament of Matrimony," she said. "I know that as Papa is my Guardian, he has to give his permission before I can be legally married while I am still a minor."

She took a deep breath before she went on:

"I therefore refuse to allow you to ... intimidate me or to ... force me to ... marry a man I have not even ... seen or ... spoken to."

"You will have plenty of time for that after you are married," Isobel retorted.

Now there was a jeering note in her voice that Safina did not miss.

Trying to think clearly, she attempted to use another tactic:

"Please, Stepmama," she said, "do not let us . . . quarrel over this, and let me . . . wait at least . . . until Papa has . . . returned from Scotland . . . before my . . . marriage is . . . discussed."

She thought for a moment that Isobel might listen to her.

Then her Stepmother said harshly:

"I will offer you an alternative. Either you marry the Duke as arranged, or else I will take you to the nearest Lunatic Asylum, and as your Guardian in your father's absence have you admitted because you are insane."

Safina felt she could not be hearing Isobel properly.

She had read about the horrors that took place in Lunatic Asylums and how harshly the patients were treated.

Even to contemplate staying a night amongst people who were mad was terrifying.

She realised it would be weeks before her father returned, and even then Isobel might not tell him where she was.

It was obvious she intended to dispose of her one way or another.

"Why are you doing this?" she asked almost pitifully.

"Because I do not want you on my hands," Isobel said. "Who would want to chaperon an unfledged girl of eighteen when I am young and enjoying life as the most beautiful woman in England."

"If that is the reason," Safina said, "then I will go away. I will not bother you, Stepmama. I will live with one of my relations. I am sure Aunt Mary will have me, or perhaps Uncle Gregory."

"And have them say I do not do my duty by you?" Isobel asked. "You are certainly crazy to think your father would allow that."

She paused for a moment.

"No, Safina, I have found an excellent way to get you out of my hair, and you ought to be thanking me on your knees that you are marrying a Duke and not a crossing-sweeper!"

"Why must I be . . . married?" Safina asked. "Let me go back to . . . the Convent. I will become . . . a Nun and will not bother you . . . again."

"And what do you think your father is going to say to that?" Isobel enquired. "No, Safina, you will do as you are told. You will marry the Duke and be thankful you do not have a worse husband!"

Her voice rose a little and was sarcastic as she went on:

"Perhaps it will cheer you up to know that he is as reluctant as you are. He is in love with the French Ambassadress, and he will therefore doubtless dislike you as much as you dislike him."

"Then . . . why is he . . . marrying me?" Safina asked.

"Because he has to obey me as you have to," Isobel replied.

"But surely . . ."

"Shut up, Safina!" Isobel snapped. "Talking is not going to change anything. As I have said, you have a choice: If you prefer the Lunatic Asylum, that is where I will take you! But make no mistake, nobody—and that includes your father—will know where you are or what has happened to you!"

She seemed almost to spit the words.

Safina put up her hand to her forehead.

She felt as if she were, in fact, going mad and was only imagining this conversation was taking place.

"Actually," Isobel went on, "I am being remarkably merciful. There are some consolations, if not many, in being the Duchess of Dallwyn."

She gave an unpleasant little laugh before she said:

"The Duke has no money, so you will not be at all comfortable. But what you do have at the moment will perhaps keep the Duns away for a little while."

Scornfully she added:

"Let us make it quite clear: If you appeal to your father to give you more money, I will prevent it. I am a young woman, and when your father dies I shall require every penny I have been able to extract from him to live in the manner to which I am now accustomed."

Safina did not answer.

She had always known that Isobel was an unpleasant woman.

Now she was aware that she was also wicked and evil.

It was impossible to think of her in her mother's place as her father's wife.

Because she had been taught ever since she was small to control herself, she bit back the words that came to her lips.

Instead, she clasped her hands together and tried to pray.

"Help me . . . oh God . . . help me!"

They were now travelling very fast along the main road.

They drove perhaps for an hour in complete silence.

Only when Isobel drew a tiny pot of salve from her reticule and started to smooth it on her lips did Safina guess they were nearing their destination.

She wondered if when the carriage came to a standstill she would be able to jump out and run away.

Then she was sure if she did so, Isobel would send the servants to catch her.

That would be very humiliating.

As she was thinking about it, the horses turned through some large wrought-iron gates.

There were lodges on either side of them, but they looked empty and in a bad state of repair.

The horses were now moving up an avenue of oak trees.

Without even looking, Safina knew that at the far end there would be the house belonging to the Duke of Dallwyn.

The man she was to marry.

'Help me . . . God . . . please . . . please . . . help me . . . save me . . . save me!'

It was a cry that came from the very depths of her heart.

But she knew even as she prayed that it was hopeless and that even God had forsaken her.

chapter three

THE horses drew up at the front-door and Safina thought she might have a last chance of escaping.

Then, as the footman got down from the box, she saw that he was young and doubtless a good runner.

If she ran away, she would be easily caught.

The Countess stepped out.

Her crimson dress and cloak looked incongruous against the ancient grey stones of the house.

Her high-heeled shoes crushed the weeds sprouting through the cracked steps which led up to the front-door.

Because there was nothing else she could do, Safina followed.

Her heart was beating frantically and her lips were dry.

She felt as if she were going to the guillotine.

An old Butler with white hair greeted them.

"Where is His Lordship?" the Countess asked sharply.

"In th' Chapel, M'Lady," the Butler replied.

"Show us the way."

It was an order, and Safina looked desperately at the stairs curving up to the next floor.

If she ran up them, it would be impossible for the Butler, who was old and somewhat unsteady on his feet, to follow her.

Then she knew that her Stepmother would somehow contrive to have her dragged back.

They walked down a long passage.

To Safina it was ominously dark, and they might have been going into the bowels of Hades.

She was praying, saying over and over again beneath her breath:

"Save me . . . please . . . save me . . . God."

She remembered how when she had parted from Sister Benedict the Nun had said:

"May God and His Angels guard you."

It was certainly something which was not happening at the moment.

She felt as if she were engulfed in a nightmare and it could not be real.

How could she—her father's daughter—be forced into marrying a man she had never even seen?

It suddenly struck her that perhaps he was old and grotesque.

Perhaps he was evil and looked like Satan.

Her Stepmother was determined to have her own way.

She was not in the least concerned with her feelings, Safina thought, and the Duke must be as bad as she was if he was prepared to yield to her orders.

How could he be so subservient to her Stepmother? How could he have no will of his own?

Then, she thought cynically, it must be because one day she would be rich.

Her mother's money would be spent by a man whom she would hate and despise.

They reached the end of the passage.

At the end there was a large door which was open.

Beyond it, Safina knew, was the Chapel.

She felt a terror rising within her.

She knew it would be impossible to make the responses.

How could she, in this mockery of a wedding which was a sin against God?

As they reached the door, the Butler stood to one side and the Countess swept in.

Safina followed her, not daring to look ahead to see the man who was waiting for her.

The Countess walked up the short aisle.

There was a smile of satisfaction on her face when she saw the Duke standing in front of the Altar steps.

Behind him was his Private Chaplain.

There were six candles lit on the Altar but there were no flowers.

Like the house, the Chapel was badly in need of restoration.

There were cracks in the stained-glass window and some of the panes of glass were missing.

The Cross on the Altar wanted polishing, and the Altar Cloth, which had once been a beautiful example of Elizabethan needlework, was faded and torn.

The Duke had turned round as the Countess approached.

When she reached him she said with a note of triumph in her voice:

"As you see, we are here."

The Duke did not speak, he merely looked at her and held out his hand.

She knew what he wanted, and for a moment she hesitated.

The Duke guessed she was thinking that at the last moment he might save himself by tearing up the letters and repudiating the agreement.

Then she knew that he was too much of a gentleman to break his word.

Reluctantly, because they had served her well, she pulled the letters from her reticule.

It was made of the same material as her gown.

The Duke took the letters from her, glanced at them, and put them in the inside pocket of his coat.

Then the Countess walked to the carved chair that stood in the Chancel.

It was intended for a Bishop or a visiting Priest.

The Duke also turned, not towards Safina but towards the Altar.

She had stopped a few feet behind her Step-mother.

Now, when she did not move, the Chaplain looked towards her, saying in a quiet voice:

"Will you stand beside the Bridegroom?"

Words of protest came to her lips, a last plea that she need not be married.

Then, as if she were aware of what she was thinking, Isobel rose from the chair in which she was sitting.

She stood looking at Safina with an expression that told her all too clearly what she would do if she did not obey.

It was then Safina realised that she was in a consecrated place.

In a Chapel dedicated to God, where she could not make an ugly scene.

If she ran away, Isobel would have her brought back, and if she protested, no one would listen.

If the Duke had agreed to this outrageous scheme, he and her Stepmother would force her into submission.

Slowly, every step forward an agony, she moved to stand next to the Duke.

She had not dared look at him since she had come into the Chapel.

She had watched the handing over of papers to him by her Stepmother, which she presumed had something to do with the marriage.

Now that she stood next to him she was aware he was vibrating with anger.

'How can Stepmama do this to us both?' she wondered.

Then, because the Duke was so tall and over-powering, she felt weak and helpless.

She was utterly alone.

Her father had no idea this was happening and, if her mother knew, she could not help her from Heaven.

"If he is as horrible as he must be," she said in her heart, "let me . . . join you Mama . . . let me die . . . because I cannot . . . live with . . . a man . . . of whom I am . . . afraid."

The Chaplain began the service.

He was an old man who knew the words by heart, and he barely glanced at his Prayer Book.

He said the prayers with a deep sincerity.

It made Safina wonder how he could speak as if he cared.

He was at the same time joining together two strangers by a bond which would shackle them for a life of misery and frustration.

Then, as if she had become a puppet with no will of her own, Safina heard herself repeating the responses after the Chaplain.

Then a ring was put on her finger.

She realised it was not a wedding-ring, but a signet ring.

The Duke must have taken it from his little finger.

Even so, it was too large and she had to close her fingers to keep it in place.

Then came the Blessing.

She wondered how any man dedicated to God could pronounce them Blessed in the circumstances.

As the Duke rose to his feet and Safina did the same, she looked at her Stepmother.

She knew from the expression in Isobel's eyes and the smile on her red lips that she was delighted she had won.

She was triumphant, ready to crow over those who had been forced to obey her.

The Chaplain was kneeling in front of the Altar.

Then to Safina's surprise the Duke took hold of her arm.

He marched her down the aisle and out through the door into the passage.

His grip hurt, and as he walked quickly she felt as if he propelled her forcibly from the Chapel.

Outside, he stopped, and she realised he was waiting for her Stepmother to join them.

Isobel did not hurry, walking lightly and with a contrived grace.

It made her seem to be acting as if on a stage.

The red feathers in her hat fluttered against

the lighted candles on the Altar and the sunshine coming through the stained-glass window.

To Safina they seemed like the fires of Hell.

She felt that her Stepmother was positively a disciple of the Devil.

The Countess reached the Duke and said in a caressing tone:

"Congratulations, dearest Crispin, and of course I hope you and Safina will be very happy."

"Leave my house!" he interrupted. "Go now and I hope I never have to see you or speak to you again!"

He spoke harshly.

At the same time, there was an authority and dignity about him which surprised Safina.

"If you mean that," Isobel replied, "it is a very stupid attitude and one which you should be well aware will react unfavourably against you."

"I am not concerned with any reaction that happens to me," the Duke retorted. "I wish only to be rid of you."

"Which is something you will find impossible," Isobel said. "Have you not forgotten that Albert will believe you have married his daughter because you fell in love with her?"

She smiled at him before she continued:

"That is also the story which I intend to circulate in London. Otherwise, as you must know, there will be some very unpleasant things said about Safina being obliged to marry in such unseemly haste."

It took a moment for Safina to understand what her Stepmother implied.

Then she was aware that the Duke had stiffened, and she gave a little gasp.

"I am leaving now," Isobel went on lightly, "because I am returning to London, and also because I am sure you young people want to be alone. Of course I shall be thinking of you, and when Albert returns, we must have a delightful family reunion where you can both tell him how happy you are!"

She accentuated the word *happy*.

Then, without waiting for the Duke to reply, she walked away down the passage, moving with an unhurried grace towards the hall.

The Duke did not move, nor did he speak, but Safina was aware that he was cursing her Stepmother under his breath.

They stood there without moving until she was out of sight.

Safina was almost afraid to breathe.

Now for the first time she looked at the man she had married.

She could see his face in profile.

It was dark in the passage and he seemed very large and as frightening as he had been in the Chapel.

He was, however, certainly not old, nor was he disfigured in any way.

At the same time, she knew he was angry and his feelings seemed to pulsate towards her.

She wanted to run away and hide.

She felt as she had when as a child she had been terrified of a thunderstorm.

Her father had found her on the floor underneath his bed with her hands over her ears.

He had picked her up in his arms and she cried against his shoulder, saying:

"There's a . . . big Ogre and he's . . . coming to . . . eat me . . . up."

The Earl had laughed.

"No, my dearest," he said, "no-one shall do that. It is only the clouds like noisy boys banging into each other."

"I'm . . . frightened," Safina sobbed.

"I will protect you," her father said, "but because you are my daughter, you have to be brave as your ancestors have been brave all down the ages."

He had told her so many stories about the battles the Wicks had fought and won.

She had seen the medals they had earned and the flags they had captured.

These were tattered but still hung over the mantelpiece in the hall.

"They did not run away from the noise of the cannon-balls," her father said, "so how can you run away from the bangs the thunder makes?"

After that Safina had always tried to be brave.

But if her father was not there to put his arms around her, she would pull the sheets and blankets over her head and hide at the bottom of her bed.

"I must be brave," she told herself now.

"Follow me," the Duke said curtly.

He began to walk ahead down the passage, but slowly, as if he were afraid of overtaking Isobel.

There was no sign of her when they reached the hall.

The Duke passed through it and went down another corridor until he opened the door.

As soon as she entered the room, Safina guessed it was his Study.

It was in some ways very like the one her father always used at Wick Park.

When, however, she looked a little closer, she was aware it was, in fact, very different.

Everything at her home, which had been decorated and arranged by her mother, was, she thought, perfection.

If a curtain faded, it was immediately replaced.

The cushions and covers on the chairs were changed every few years.

Here was a very different story.

The leather sofa and armchairs were of the same design as those used by her father, but the leather was faded and torn.

The carpet and rugs on which the furniture stood were thread-bare.

There were stains on the ceiling and on the walls too.

The Duke walked to the fireplace and stood with his back to it.

"Sit down."

It was an order rather than a request, and Safina sat quickly on the nearest chair.

It was an upright one, and having sat down, she looked at the Duke.

Now she was surprised to see he was, in fact, very good-looking.

His square shoulders and narrow hips told her he was athletic.

As she was looking at him for the first time, so was he looking at her.

He was thinking she was not the least that he had expected.

He had been somehow sure that the unfledged girl Isobel was thrusting on him would be exactly like the *débutantes* he had seen in London.

Pretty in an insipid way, fair-haired, blue-eyed, and either giggling or too shy to say anything.

Instead, he found himself looking at a young woman who did not resemble anyone he had ever seen before.

It struck him that she was not pretty.

But she had a face that seemed to him vaguely familiar, although he could not think why.

She had almost classical features.

Her hair, instead of being fair, was the indefinable shade that reminded him of a pastel by Michelangelo.

She had very large eyes fringed with dark lashes.

They appeared to be grey, but because she was

frightened, there was an almost purple tinge in them.

She did not move or speak, but just sat with her back very straight, looking at him.

There was a silence in which neither of them moved until at last the Duke said:

"It is difficult to know what either of us should say in these very unusual circumstances. There is no recognised form of words in which to introduce oneself to someone one has not met before but has just married."

He was trying to invest what he felt was an infuriating situation with some semblance of dignity.

"I ... am ... sorry," Safina said in a very small voice.

"There is no reason for you to be sorry," the Duke replied, "except for yourself. I imagine you are as horrified as I am by what has just occurred."

"How could ... you have ... let it ... happen?" Safina asked.

"Let it?" the Duke exclaimed.

Then, as if he felt he had spoken too angrily, he added gently:

"I was blackmailed and forced into a position where I had to agree to what your Stepmother demanded."

"What ... can we ... do about ... it?"

Now her voice was hardly audible.

The Duke thought she was controlling herself and her fear in what was an admirable manner.

He walked across the room and back again to the fireplace before he said:

"Quite frankly, there is nothing we can do but accept the situation and try, if it is humanly possible, to make the best of it."

"Do you . . . mean I have . . . to remain . . . married to . . . you?"

"We are married," the Duke said, "and there is no escape."

Safina drew in her breath.

"Stepmama told me that . . . you needed . . . my money. Perhaps she did not . . . tell you that . . . I have very little until Papa dies."

"She told me," the Duke replied, "that you have thirty thousand pounds."

He felt as he spoke that it was rather uncomfortable to talk about money so soon after they were married.

But as she had brought the subject up, perhaps it was best to know exactly where they stood.

"Mama left me . . . thirty thousand pounds . . . in her Will, but I have only . . . the income from it . . . until I am . . . twenty-five."

The Duke stared at her.

He realised that Isobel had tricked him again by saying that the thirty thousand pounds could pay his more pressing debts.

He might have expected that she would lie to get her own way.

In consequence, he was still in the same desperate position that he had been in for the past two years.

As if she understood what he was feeling, Safina said:

"I am . . . sorry. Perhaps . . . the best thing . . . I can do is what I . . . suggested to . . . Stepmama."

"What was that?" the Duke asked.

"That . . . I should go . . . back to . . . Florence and . . . become a Nun."

"And what did your Stepmother reply to that?" the Duke enquired.

"She said that . . . when he . . . heard about it, Papa would not . . . allow it . . . to happen, so I . . . had to marry . . . you."

"And did you tell her you had no wish to marry a stranger?"

As Safina did not answer at once, he added:

"Perhaps you felt it would be rather pleasant to become a Duchess?"

There was a note of cynicism in his voice, and Safina replied:

"Of course I had . . . no wish whatever to . . . marry you! I think it is . . . wicked to be . . . married when . . . we are both . . . hating each . . . other!"

She drew in her breath before she added:

"I wanted . . . desperately to say I . . . would not . . . do it, but Stepmama . . . threatened what she would do if I did not, and . . . it was . . . too . . . horrifying."

"How did she threaten you?" the Duke enquired.

He thought for a moment that Safina was not going to answer. Then she replied:

"She said if I . . . refused in the . . . Chapel . . . she would make the servants . . . hold me until I responded, and if I did not . . . agree to . . . come here she would . . . take me to . . . a Lunatic Asylum and have me . . . certified as . . . insane."

The Duke gave an exclamation that seemed to ring out in the room.

"Curse her! How can she behave in such a diabolical manner? Or we be helpless to do anything about it?"

"I . . . was afraid," Safina said, "that if she . . . put me in an . . . Asylum no-one would . . . know where I . . . was and I might have to . . . stay there . . . all my life!"

The Duke put his hand to his forehead.

"We have both been trapped," he said, "and all I can say is that I hope one day your Stepmother gets her just desserts."

There was silence as he stood at the window looking out on the overgrown garden.

He was fighting for his self-control as Safina had fought for hers.

He thought that only a woman as unprincipled as Isobel could threaten a girl with being certified as a lunatic.

He supposed that, as Safina's Guardian, this was something which she could do quite easily.

It would be such a horrifying experience that

it could make a young, well-bred girl actually insane.

"She is totally evil," the Duke told himself.

He was ashamed to think he had ever suc-cumbed to her sensual and fiery desires.

In retrospect, he thought they were, in fact, abnormal.

"Would it not be ... best for ... me to go ... back to ... Florence?" Safina asked.

The Duke was startled by the concern in her voice and walked back towards the fireplace.

"No, of course not!" he said. "To begin with, I cannot believe you want to renounce the world. You may find the situation in which you now are in uncomfortable and unpleasant, but per-haps we can eventually be able to do something about it."

"You mean you ... want to ... restore your house and make it ... beautiful as it ... must have been ... originally?"

"Of course I want that," the Duke said almost roughly, "but I have as much chance of doing so as jumping over the moon or finding a crock of gold at the end of the rainbow."

"I am afraid what ... money I have got ... will not go very ... far," Safina said, "and if I ask for ... any of the rest of the money which was ... Mama's, my Stepmother has ... already said that ... she will prevent Papa from ... giving it to me."

"That is one thing of which you can be quite certain," the Duke remarked. "Your Stepmother is a young woman, and she intends before your father dies to get as much money as possible into her possession."

"Yes, I know . . . that," Safina said, "and I do not . . . even have any . . . of Mama's jewels which she . . . always told me were . . . mine."

"Then it is no use crying over spilt milk," the Duke said. "I warn you, you will be uncomfortable and it would not surprise me if sometimes you were hungry. All I can offer you is a roof over your head, even if it leaks!"

To his surprise, Safina laughed.

"I am . . . sorry! I ought . . . not to laugh . . . at you," she said, "but it sounds . . . so ridiculous that . . . you are a Duke and own this enormous house . . . acres of land, but have . . . no money."

"Just debts," the Duke said, "and if I am not careful, I will find myself in a debtors' prison."

"How can it possibly be as bad as that?" Safina enquired.

"If you can find anything in this house to sell," the Duke replied, "I will sell it. As you may imagine, everything is entailed onto the son I do not possess, and anything that is saleable has already gone!"

"What are you going to do?" Safina asked.

"I have not the faintest idea," the Duke replied. "It is bad enough trying to keep myself and two old servants who have nowhere else to go but the Workhouse. Now I have also a wife like an Albatross around my neck!"

After he had spoken he said quickly:

"I apologise, I was not intending to be rude. I am only stating crude facts."

"I am not offended," Safina said. "At least we have the income from my capital until I am twenty-five."

"We?" the Duke asked. "Are you really allying yourself with me in this appalling situation?"

Safina looked at him a little uncertainly.

"Is there . . . anything else you can . . . suggest that I . . . can do?" she asked tentatively.

"If you want to be comfortable," the Duke said, "you could doubtless find yourself a home with one of your relations."

"I cannot for the moment think of one that would want me," Safina answered, "and surely it would cause a great deal of . . . gossip if we lived apart . . . immediately after we were . . . married?"

"That is true," the Duke said, "but I was just thinking how unpleasant it would be for you here."

"And for . . . you," Safina said in a small voice.

"I agree to that, though it sounds extremely rude," he said. "May I now say before we get any further that you are not the least what I expected."

"What did you expect?" Safina asked.

"To be honest," the Duke replied, "I thought you would be either hysterical or coy."

Safina laughed.

"I did feel hysterical when Stepmama told me what she had planned, and again when I . . . came into . . . the Chapel."

She hesitated before she added:

"I thought you might be . . . very old and perhaps . . . deformed or . . . evil."

"I hope, at any rate, I am none of those things," the Duke replied.

"No, you . . . certainly are not," Safina assured him.

Without really thinking what she was doing, and concentrating on their conversation, she pulled off her hat.

She put it down on the ground beside her chair.

The Duke saw that her hair was parted at the centre and swept back into a bun at the back of her head.

There were two curls falling down on either side of her heart-shaped face.

Her forehead was a perfect oval.

As he looked at her straight nose and again at her large, very eloquent eyes, he gave an exclamation.

"Now I know what you look like!"

"What is that?"

"The pictures of some of the very young Italian Madonnas in the Uffizi Gallery."

Safina stared at him.

"Do . . . you mean . . . that? I have . . . looked at . . . them a thousand times and . . . longed to be . . . like them."

"Your wish has been granted," he said, "and uncannily so."

He smiled, and it seemed to transform his face.

"Perhaps, after all, you are not my wife, but an Angel from Heaven, who will disappear back to where you came from."

"I wish . . . that were true," Safina said, "and then . . . perhaps you could . . . be happy."

She stopped herself from saying more.

The Duke made a gesture with his hand and walked back again to the window.

"That is something which is impossible," he said, "until I can clear up the mess I am in."

"I will help you! I am sure I can . . . help you in . . . some way," Safina said, "even though I do not have as much . . . money as you . . . expected me . . . to have."

"I did not consider that when I refused to marry you," he said harshly. "I told your Stepmother I was not prepared to sell my title."

So he had not wanted her money.

Now Safina was sure that the reason why he had been forced to marry her had something to do with the papers which her Stepmother had given him in the Chapel.

She wanted to ask him what they were.

Then she feared he might resent her seeming to pry into his affairs.

Perhaps sooner or later he would tell her why he had been unable to defy the Countess.

The Duke turned from the window.

"I think it must be nearly luncheon-time," he said, "and I suggest that I take you upstairs and show you your bedroom."

He paused before adding:

"I am afraid there will be no-one to wait on you."

Safina realised for the first time that when she and her stepmother left the Inn where they had spent the night, the maids had been left behind.

She had presumed that they had gone to London in the other carriage.

She had not given it a thought until now.

Her trunks must have been transferred to the carriage in which she had come here.

"After luncheon," the Duke said, "I will take you on an inspection of the house, and you will see how by neglect a building can gradually become nothing but a pile of stones."

He spoke bitterly, and Safina answered:

"I am sure it is not as bad as that, and I have just thought of something we ought to do."

"What is that?" the Duke asked.

It was obvious from his tone that he thought it unlikely that any idea she had would be of any use.

Suddenly she felt shy about what she had been about to say:

"I would . . . like to see . . . over the house," she said, "and of course . . . your gardens and . . . your estate. How large is it?"

The Duke realised that that was not what she had been going to say.

But he was not really interested.

He was only thinking that, while Safina was not as bad as he had expected, Isobel had won.

She had defeated him as she had determined to do.

Now she would gloat over the torture of his being tied to a wife with whom he was not in love, torture which she had envisaged from the very start.

She had been well aware that Safina would not have enough money to be of any real help for another seven years!

chapter four

AFTER a very sparse and, Safina thought, almost uneatable luncheon, the Duke said:

"Now I will take you around the house and you will see what I have to endure day after day!"

There was a bitterness in his voice which Safina realised was always there when he talked of his possessions.

He took her first into the rooms on the ground floor which, it was obvious, had once been as magnificent as those at Wick.

Now everything was faded or thread-bare.

Water had seeped through the ceilings, ruining those which were painted.

Every room they visited needed repairing from the ceiling to the floor.

The only things that were untouched were the

eighteenth-century marble mantelpieces.

However, where the rooms had had fires the ashes were still in the grates.

In the Ballroom, because the chimney had not been swept, there was a horrifying mess.

The soot had fallen down onto the polished floor.

Safina had to admit the inspection was gloomy.

The Duke spoke very little.

When he did, the bitterness in his voice and the pain in his eyes made her desperately sorry for him.

She knew she was right in thinking that the income she received from her present capital would merely be a drop in the ocean.

A fortune was required to restore the house to what it had been originally.

Of course, the money was there.

Her mother's fortune was enormous.

To restore the House, the Garden, and the Estate would not noticeably deplete what would be hers on her father's death.

On the first floor they went from State Room to State Room.

The huge four-posters, canopied beds with curtains falling from a gold corona, must have at one time been very lovely.

Now it was difficult to appreciate them, as everything was so shabby.

There were panes of glass missing in the windows, and in some rooms the curtains were in rags.

Of course there was dust everywhere.

It would have been impossible, as Safina knew, for the old couple to cope.

As the only servants the Duke had left, they could only try to cook him what food was available.

Banks was over seventy-five and his wife was only a year or two younger.

Safina gathered that they had seldom gone farther than from the Kitchen to the Dining Room and the hall.

The rest of the house had to look after itself.

'At least,' she thought to herself, 'I can pay for several younger servants.'

It was obviously essential to have someone to assist Mrs. Banks in the Kitchen.

Safina was also thinking that she must buy food not only for the Duke and herself, but also for the servants.

When they had finished what was only a quick inspection of the House, the Duke took Safina to the Stables.

It was equally painful to see how the roof had fallen in in several places.

The stalls which had once been spacious and worthy of fine horse-flesh were filled with dirty straw and manure.

The Duke had two horses, both of which were getting old.

Safina saw they were in need of grooming.

"I used to have a boy from the Village to help me," the Duke said as if she had asked the question, "but he got a better-paid job, and who should blame him?"

They walked from the Stables back into the court-yard in front of the House.

Safina looked at the long drive up which she had driven the previous day.

The trees on each side of it were old, but she thought, they at least, because they were Oaks, seemed to be flourishing.

There was a lake directly below the House, and she saw there were several ducks on it.

"There used to be swans," the Duke said as he followed the direction of her eyes, "but they flew away because they were hungry. The ducks, as you can imagine, are a benefit for which I am extremely grateful."

"You are not shooting at the moment?" Safina asked quickly.

She had realised before she spoke that several of the ducks had small ducklings swimming behind them.

"No, of course not," he replied, "and we will certainly need the new additions later on in the year."

"If nothing else, the money I have will provide us with good food," Safina said, "and I was also thinking it would pay for some more servants."

The Duke looked angry.

She knew without his saying so that he was furious that he could not provide these things himself.

"If you are going to be proud," she said without thinking, "it will make things more difficult than they are already."

"Difficult is not the right word," he retorted. "Intolerable is better!"

Feeling as if he had snubbed her, she did not reply but only walked down over what had once been a lawn towards the lake.

When she reached it the Duke joined her.

She could feel the anger and frustration pouring out of him.

To change the subject, she said:

"I can see your lake is very deep. Do you ever swim here?"

"Yes, often," the Duke answered, "and it is certainly easier than trying to get a bath in the House."

Again his voice seemed raw, and Safina said:

"You are lucky. I have always wanted to swim but Mama thought it would be immodest at Wick since there were always so many people about. Of course the Nuns in Florence would have been shocked at the idea."

"Well, you will have to learn to swim here," the Duke said, "or go without a bath!"

He turned away from the lake as he spoke.

Safina stood looking at the ducks, seeing that there were more of them than she had seen from the court-yard.

She was also thinking the irises and kingcups growing thickly at the bottom of the high banks were beautiful.

Then she was aware that the Duke was walking back towards the House and turned to follow him.

Things certainly were in a terrible state, but at the same time she thought that he was making the very worst of it.

They had almost reached the Garden when she saw a large Oak Tree.

It was growing beside what had once been, she thought, a Bowling-Alley.

The tree seemed somewhat incongruous amongst weed-filled flower-beds and what she knew had been laid out as a Rose Garden.

It had a sun-dial in the centre of it.

Then, as she went on a little farther, she saw there was a woman under the Oak Tree.

The Duke had stopped to speak to her.

"Good afternoon, Mrs. Hewins," he said, "were you wanting to see me?"

"No, yer Grace, Oi comes 'ere t' get a few leaves from th' Magic Tree for m' daughter."

She paused before continuing:

" 'Er be getting married tomorrow 'nd th' one thing 'er says 'er wants better than any present be th' leaves that 'ill bring 'er good luck an' make sure 'er has fine babies."

As Safina reached the Duke she saw he was smiling.

"Do you really believe, Mrs. Hewins," he said, "that the leaves of King Charles' Oak will do all that?"

"Oh, it does, Yer Grace," Mrs. Hewins said positively. "It saved me 'usband last year when th' doctor despaired of 'im, an' when Mary Chance—Yer Grace remembers 'er?—had been married for six years without a baby an' had one nine months to th' day after 'er carried one o' th' Oak leaves in 'er breast."

Mrs. Hewins paused for breath, then she added:

"Four children 'er 'as now, three sons an' a daughter, all due 'er says t' Yer Grace's Magic Oak leaves!"

The Duke laughed.

"Well, you are certainly a convincing enthusiast for them, Mrs. Hewins. Please give your daughter my good wishes."

Mrs. Hewins bobbed a curtsy.

"Oi'll tell 'er what yer says, Yer Grace, an' very pleased 'er'll be an' grateful too for what Oi'll be takin' for 'er from th' tree."

"Help yourself," the Duke said, "and of course that goes for anybody else in the village."

They walked on towards the House, and as Safina moved beside him she said:

"Tell me about the tree, and why it is magical."

"That is what they believe locally," he said, "but it certainly has not brought me any luck!"

"You said it was King Charles' Tree. Do you mean Charles II?"

"My Ancestor, the third Earl of Dallwyn, was a staunch Royalist," the Duke replied.

"What happened?" Safina questioned.

"When the Restoration came and King Charles

II came to the throne, one of the first places he visited was Wyn Park."

"How interesting," Safina murmured, "I do wish I had been here then."

"When I was a boy I used to wish the same," the Duke replied. "Apparently there were great feastings and festivities, and before he left, King Charles planted the Oak."

Safina glanced back at it as the Duke spoke, and he went on:

"It is reported that His Majesty said:

" 'You have brought me luck, Dallwyn, and I therefore plant this tree, hoping it will bring you luck and everyone else who shelters under it.' "

The Duke paused before he said:

"I doubt that those were his actual words, but my family and those who live on the Estate believe them literally. They believe that the leaves on King Charles' Oak will solve all of their problems."

"And do they?" Safina asked.

"You heard what Mrs. Hewins said," the Duke answered, "but though I own the tree, it has done nothing for me."

Now he was being bitter again, and Safina felt it was not surprising.

When they reached the House there seemed to be no question of their having any tea.

She was therefore glad when the Duke suggested that they should dine early.

"There will not be much to eat," he said, "and as the Bankses like to go to bed early, I usually have something at seven o'clock."

"That will suit me," Safina said.

She went to her room and walked to her window.

"At least I have a magnificent view," she told herself.

The sun was sinking and at the same time was turning the lake to gold.

There was a crimson glow behind the Oak Trees.

'It could all be so beautiful if only he had enough money,' Safina thought.

It struck her that to endure seven years of listening to the Duke's bitterness and frustration would make her very unhappy.

"I am sure I can persuade Papa to give me some money," she said aloud.

But she knew she was being over-optimistic and forgetting her Stepmother.

She remembered, too, that the Duke was not only bitter because of his House.

If Isobel was to be believed, he was in love with the French Ambassador's wife.

"I must talk to him sometime as to whether we stay here indefinitely or go to London," she told herself.

She thought it might be easier if they did not have the gloom of dilapidation staring at them all the time.

She felt, however, it was too soon for her to discuss his movements.

Nor should she ask him whether he had any

plans as to what they could do.

'It is not quite as frightening as I thought,' she decided, 'and there is one thing we must have—that is horses!'

She thought her father would not refuse to give her some from his very large Stables.

Even her Stepmother would not prevent that.

She changed into one of the simple evening-gowns she had bought in Florence.

As she did so, she thought that Wyn Park and the Duke were a challenge.

She felt as if her mother were telling her that she had to do something about them both.

"You will have to help me, Mama," she said. "It is not going to be easy, and I feel he will resent my help because I am a wife he does not want."

She had to unpack her own gown for the evening.

She found in her bedroom the two trunks she had brought with her from Florence.

She was certain that Banks would not have been able to carry them upstairs.

He must have persuaded her Stepmother's Coachman and footman to do so before they left.

Otherwise, she told herself, she would have had to unpack in the hall or ask the Duke to bring them upstairs.

Now there was another problem which she would have to solve one way or another.

When her trunks were empty, somebody would have to take them away.

She looked at herself in the mirror and thought that perhaps the Duke would admire her dress.

It was made of the beautiful Florentine silk which was the finest in Italy.

Safina had, however, deliberately not bought many gowns before she left.

As she was to be a *débutante,* she was sure her father would wish her to buy a great number of gowns from the best dressmakers in London.

The clothes she had were what she had worn for her last year at School, with the addition of just three or four dresses she had purchased so that she would not look too dowdy on her first days at home.

"Perhaps I shall eventually be as dilapidated and thread-bare as the House," she told her reflection, "but I will try not to be bitter about it."

She walked downstairs with her head held high and found the Duke waiting for her in the Study.

It was still only April, so someone—she suspected it was the Duke himself—had lit a fire in the grate.

It was smoking a little, as if the chimney was dirty, but it made the room seem more cheerful.

Then as she looked at the Duke she saw he had changed for dinner.

Despite the fact that his cut-away coat showed signs of wear, he looked very smart.

To her surprise, when she joined him at the

fireplace he handed her a glass.

"Champagne!" Safina exclaimed.

"You will hardly believe it," he answered, "but apparently your Stepmother left behind the bottle and what remained of the food she carried with her on your journey here."

He gave a short laugh before he went on:

"I think she meant to be insulting, but personally I am thankful for small mercies, this wine being one of them!"

As he finished speaking, he raised his glass.

"To a reluctant Bride," he said, "whom I must commend for the very brave way she has confronted what must seem an incredible marriage."

"Thank you," Safina answered. "I must respond with my good wishes to a reluctant Bridegroom."

They both drank a little from their glasses, and then the Duke said:

"Now I will take you in to Dinner, and I will bring the bottle with us. We must not waste anything so delicious!"

"Of course not," Safina agreed.

They walked along the passage and across the hall to the Dining Room.

Banks was waiting for them.

Safina realised he had made a tremendous effort and brought out some of the silver for the occasion.

There were four Georgian Candlesticks which had obviously been cleaned very hastily.

There was a large Silver Rose Bowl in the centre of the table in which he had arranged rather clumsily some white flowers.

"It looks lovely!" she exclaimed. "Thank you for making my first dinner here so attractive."

Banks was delighted.

As the Duke and Safina sat down, he shuffled away to bring them their food.

There was, thanks to Isobel, an excellent *pâté* that Safina had eaten the previous night.

It was followed by nearly half a cold salmon which she thought had also been in the hamper.

For dessert there was a pudding which was not very appetising.

It had obviously been made by Mrs. Banks with the few ingredients she had.

As Banks took away the plates, he said in what was meant to be a whisper to the Duke:

"That be all, Yer Grace, us ain't got anythin' else to eat."

"I hope you and Mrs. Banks will enjoy what is left of the *pâté* and the salmon," the Duke said.

Safina saw the old man's face light up.

They had obviously expected that what was left had to be kept for what they called "the gentry."

"One thing is quite obvious," Safina said as soon as Banks had left the room, "we shall either have to go shopping tomorrow, or you will have to go shooting!"

She saw his lips tighten, as if he were annoyed at there being so little in the House.

Then he said:

"I expect, being a woman, you will want to take over the Kitchen if nothing else."

"I will certainly try," Safina answered, "and actually I myself can cook."

The Duke raised his eyebrows.

"Is that really one of the subjects taught at a Finishing School?"

"Not to all the pupils," Safina answered, "but because Papa was, as he said himself, an epicure and gourmet, we always had a very talented Chef at Wick."

She saw the Duke was listening, and she went on:

"I was only five when I first tried to cook because it fascinated me and I was always hanging about the Kitchen. To keep me out of their way, the Chefs would give me some ingredients to work at a table by myself."

She smiled as she went on:

"Later Mama built me a Wendy House with a stove on which I could cook dishes for her and my Governesses."

"Well, that is certainly a way you can earn your living if all else fails," the Duke said. "Unfortunately I have no saleable talents."

"How can you be certain of that?" Safina asked. "I am sure you are a good rider, so you could become a Riding-Master or perhaps a Shooting-Instructor."

"And how much would I earn in either of those capacities?" the Duke asked. "Not enough to pay for the dinner we have just eaten."

He was back to being dismal again, and Safina rose to her feet.

"If there is no port for you to drink," she said, "you had better bring your glass and what is left in the champagne bottle to the Study. We can go on talking in front of the fire."

She thought, as she spoke, that it was cold in the Dining-Room.

She decided that another night she would bring a wrap downstairs with her.

She suspected that behind the drawn curtains there were broken panes of glass that let in the wind.

The Dining-Room itself was large enough to seat forty people without their being crowded.

The Duke did not reply, but followed her from the Dining-Room, carrying the bottle of champagne and two glasses.

When, however, they reached the Study, Safina said she wanted no more to drink, she was feeling sleepy already.

"I hope you will sleep well," the Duke said. "If nothing else, the mattresses in this House are made of the best goose-feathers and are therefore extremely comfortable."

As he finished speaking, he sat down and said:

"I think, Safina, you have behaved with admirable composure today and, as I said in my toast, you have been very brave."

"Thank you," Safina replied. "I think we have both been commendably dignified."

"I was thinking when I was dressing," the Duke said, "that the best thing we can do is to behave as naturally as possible."

"Yes, of course," Safina agreed, "and though it seems impossible at the moment, perhaps things will not be quite so difficult as they appear to be."

"You are certainly optimistic," the Duke answered.

She thought he was mocking her and rose to her feet.

"I think I will go to bed."

"Of course," the Duke agreed.

He drank what was left in his glass and put the guard in front of the fire.

He blew out the candles which had been lit on each side of the mantelpiece.

The curtains had not been drawn, and it was dusk outside.

The first evening-star was struggling to glitter in the sky over the top of the trees.

Safina realised that he was going to come upstairs with her.

She therefore waited until he joined her at the door she held open.

It was dark in the passage outside.

There were two candle-sticks on the table in the hall and one of the candles had been lit.

The Duke lit the other one and they walked up the stairs side by side.

They moved along a wide passage.

Safina noticed for the first time that there were several fine inlaid chests underneath portraits of the Duke's Ancestors.

They had obviously been painted by the Master of each period.

The pictures needed cleaning, the chests dusting.

At the same time, there was something charming and elegant about them which pleased her.

The Duke stopped outside her door.

Then as she was about to say goodnight, he said:

"I hope you have everything you want. I shall not be long, and there is a communicating-door between our rooms which you may not have noticed."

He did not wait for her reply but walked on a little farther to open the door of his own bedroom.

Safina stared after him in astonishment.

She felt she must have misunderstood him. Yet he had said definitely that he would "not be long."

She went into her own room, put down the candle, and stared at a door she had not noticed before.

It was near the window, and it obviously opened into the next room.

'Could . . . he possibly . . . mean . . . ?'

Then, as she faced the truth, she put her

hands up to her face as if to protect herself.

When the Duke had said he thought they should behave in a normal way, she had not thought he meant this.

How could he possibly behave as a normal husband to her when he was in love with someone else?

Safina was innocent, in as much as she had no idea actually how a man and a woman made love.

She knew if they slept together it resulted in a child, and that anything they did would be very intimate.

At the same time, if they loved each other as her mother had loved her father, it would be very wonderful.

That was very different from allowing a man she had never seen until that morning to come into her room.

He would sleep in her bed and of course touch and perhaps kiss her.

She felt her whole body revolt at the idea.

Now she was terrified as she had been in the Chapel when the Duke had seemed overpowering.

She had felt his hatred for her vibrating from him.

"He still hates me," she told herself, "but at the same time, because he is trying to behave in a dignified and normal manner, he will make me his wife!"

She knew at that moment that in such circumstances she could not bear to have a child by him.

If indeed they had one, perhaps it would be as grotesque and ugly as she had thought he might be.

"It would be a sin . . . a sin against . . . God for him to give me a baby when he loves someone else."

She knew vaguely, because the girls at School talked, that men amused themselves, even when they were married, with women like actresses.

Also, sometimes, though she was not quite sure of this, with women of their own class.

While the other girls whispered about such things, Safina was not interested.

To her, love was something beautiful—the rapture she had seen in her mother's eyes, the ecstasy she read about in the poetry, plays, and prose which she had found in the School Library.

They were tales which emphasised the spiritual side of love.

She thought it was the same as what she felt in the Chapel when the voices of the choir were like a paean of joy from the Angels.

She felt the same when she received the blessed sacrament and her heart was lifted up to God.

How could she feel that with a man who hated her and wished there were another woman in her place?

She looked at the communicating-door and knew that in a few minutes the Duke would join her.

It was then she felt sheer panic sweep over her.

She knew she must escape!

She ran across the room and opened the door into the passage very quietly.

It was dark except for a glimmer of light.

It came from the long windows in the hall over which the curtains had not been drawn.

It enabled her to find her way silently downstairs until she reached the front-door.

To her relief, it was not bolted, and the key was just turned in the lock.

It made no sound as she turned it back and the door opened.

Instantly she felt the cold of the night air on her face.

It was then she began to run across the courtyard over the lawns and down towards the lake.

She was breathless when she reached it.

The stars were coming out one by one and she could see them reflected in the still water.

It was very quiet; even the ducks had gone to sleep.

She looked at the lake stretching away from the high bank on which she stood.

She thought it was a long way to the other side.

It was then she told herself that this was her only way of escape!

Perhaps it was wrong, perhaps it was wicked—she was sure the Reverend Mother would say it was a sin.

But what was the alternative?

To go back to fight against the Duke's hatred?

Seven years had to pass before she could really be of any use to him.

Every day he would loathe her more because she had been foisted on him.

'If I . . . die,' Safina thought, 'I shall be with Mama . . . and she . . . will understand . . . that I did the . . . only thing that it was . . . possible to do.'

She thought of her stepmother and how glad she would be that she was permanently out of her way.

'She hates me, the Duke hates me, and there is . . . no-one to whom I can . . . turn for . . . help!'

She looked again at the water.

It was dark and cold and she had been so happy until she arrived in England.

'I must . . . do it . . . I must.'

Once again the panic was rising in her as she thought of the Duke going into her bedroom.

He would find that she was not there and would come in search of her.

He had seemed different this afternoon.

But now the fear that had stabbed her like a sharp knife when she was being married was making it hard to think.

She wanted to scream.

"Will . . . I scream . . . when I . . . drown?" she asked herself.

Then she remembered that someone had told her that drowning was a very pleasant way of dying.

Except that everything that has happened in your past flashes before your eyes.

'I will see Mama and Papa and Wick,' she thought, 'the horses . . . the gardens and . . . Mama telling me stories about the . . . flowers and the . . . birds.'

It was a happy thought.

It seemed to rise above the turmoil in her breast, the horror and fear of her thoughts, and the pain in her heart.

She glanced back over her shoulder.

It was difficult to see in the dim light.

But she was aware there was someone large and sinister moving down through the grass, the way she had come herself.

It was then she gave a scream which shattered the silence before she flung herself violently into the lake!

chapter five

THE Duke undressed in his room.

He was thinking it was sensible that he and Safina had agreed the only way their marriage could work was for them to behave as normally as possible.

He realised he had been somewhat disagreeable during the day, but surely it was understandable.

At least the wife that Isobel had forced upon him was intelligent.

As they had gone round the house, he soon learnt that Safina was conversant with the great artists who had painted his Ancestors' portraits.

She also had a knowledge of furniture, which surprised him.

He was most impressed with her composure

and the way she had apparently accepted what to him was an appalling situation.

When he was ready for bed he blew out the candles in his room and walked towards the communicating-door.

It was a double door because the walls were so thick.

He opened the one on his side and then groped in the darkness for the handle of Safina's door.

He walked in.

By the light of the candle which was burning by the bed he saw that she was not there.

He thought it strange and wondered where she could have gone.

The door was open into the passage.

Then, as he looked round, he realised she had not undressed.

She might have put everything she took off away in the wardrobe or the drawers, but it was unlikely.

It never entered his head that she had run away.

He thought she must have gone downstairs to fetch something.

But he could not remember anything that they had left behind.

He walked down the corridor to the top of the staircase.

As he reached it, he felt a cold draught and saw that the front-door was open.

Then it did flash through his mind that she might have run away.

Only as he went down the stairs did it strike him that perhaps she had been afraid of him.

He was so used to women falling into his arms before he hardly knew their names.

Because he was so good-looking and came from such a noble family, he had been pursued by women ever since he had left Eton.

He reached the front-door.

When he went through it, he could see in the moonlight a figure by the lake.

He could not believe at this hour of night, when it was distinctly chilly, that Safina was admiring the view.

Earlier in the day she had been thrilled by the beauty of the lake with the ducks swimming on it.

Then, as he looked at her, his instinct suddenly told him what she intended to do.

He thought at first it must be a figment of his imagination.

How could she now be hysterical when she had been calm and controlled and he had admired her serenity.

Nevertheless, he hurried down the steps and started to walk very quickly over the thick grass.

Then he saw Safina turn her head.

She must have seen him coming, for a moment later she screamed and flung herself into the lake.

The Duke started to run, and as he did so he pulled off his thick velvet dressing-gown.

He remembered that Safina had said she could not swim.

When he reached the side of the lake he did not stop to look for her in the water.

He plunged in wearing only his night-shirt.

She came to the surface just a little ahead of him and he caught hold of her.

As he did so he realised she was unconscious.

The Duke was a strong swimmer and without any difficulty he towed Safina to the side of the lake.

He lifted her over the irises and kingcups onto the ground.

Then he climbed up to join her.

Her dress clung to her body.

Her hair which had become loose in her fall was hanging limp against her wet cheeks.

Her eyes were closed.

The Duke knew she had hit the water so flatly that it had been a hard blow on her forehead.

She would doubtless be severely bruised.

He looked at her for only a few seconds.

Then he pulled off his wet night-shirt and flung it on the ground.

He picked up his dressing-gown from where he had thrown it down and put it on her.

Then he carried Safina back over the thick grass to the court-yard.

She was very light.

He could feel her wet clothes soaking through his dressing-gown.

As they went up the stairs he was aware they

were leaving a trail of water on every step.

When the Duke reached Safina's bedroom he hesitated for a moment, wondering whether he should lay her on the bed.

Instead, he put her down on the floor.

He could see by the light of the candle that she was completely oblivious of everything, and he went quickly to his own room.

He rubbed himself down with a towel and put on the first pair of trousers he could find.

He took a shirt from a drawer.

Instead of wearing it, he carried it over his arm.

He thought that if Safina came back to consciousness and saw him naked, she might be shocked.

It was something that had never occurred to him before in any of his dealings with women.

He was realising now that Safina was different and very young.

When he returned to her bedroom she was lying exactly where he had left her.

Now her wet clothes had made a dark patch on the carpet and it was spreading out on each side of her.

He put his shirt down on the bed.

Then, picking up a candle, he went to the linen-cupboard which was at the far end of the corridor.

Because he had few visitors, there were piles of sheets, pillow-cases, and towels.

They were all clean, though a large number of them needed mending.

The Duke picked up a number of towels and went back to Safina.

He lit several more candles from the one he carried.

Then, kneeling on the floor, he began to undress her.

He thought with a slight twist of his lips it was the first time he had ever undressed a woman who was completely unconscious.

As he took off her clothes, he thought her not yet mature body was very beautiful.

Her tip-tilted breasts, her tiny waist, and slender hips were faultless.

She might indeed have been one of the Madonnas she resembled except that her skin was so white.

'She is very young,' he thought again.

He knew she would be deeply shocked if she realised what he was doing.

He dried her long hair as well as he could while below the waist her chemise covered her.

Then he put three towels on the pillow in the bed and drew back the sheets and blankets.

When she was completely naked he dried her quickly, trying not to think how lovely she was.

She had run away from him because he had frightened her.

He was now worried that she would regain consciousness before he could get her into bed.

When, however, he lifted her from the floor, her head, with her long hair, which he knew now was as fine as silk, fell back limply against his chest.

He carried her to the bed.

He laid her down with her head on the towels and pulled the sheets and blankets up to her chin.

She looked very small and rather lost in the big four-poster.

He thought she was pathetic and needed to be protected, not only against the wickedness of Isobel, but also against himself.

"How could I have been such a fool," he asked himself, "as not to have understood that she would be afraid and doubtless innocent of what marriage means?"

He was angry that he had not been more perceptive.

He had prided himself on it in the past.

When he was in the Army before he inherited, he had used that perception where the men he commanded were concerned.

He had been the most popular Officer in the Household Brigade.

He turned away from the bed to pick up another fresh towel and wipe his chest and arms.

Then he put on his shirt which was lying at the end of the bed.

Carrying the wet towels he had used in drying Safina, and a candle, he left the room.

He went downstairs to the Kitchen.

He knew both the Bankses would be in bed at this hour, and he had no intention of disturbing them.

He told himself no-one must ever know what had happened.

He put the wet towels down on the table and decided he would tell Banks in the morning he had been swimming.

Banks would not be surprised, as it was something he often did.

There was still a fire burning in the stove, which was old and needed replacing.

The Duke added more fuel and filled a kettle.

Then he opened the cupboards in the Kitchen one by one.

He finally found what he was seeking, which was a stone hot-water bottle. There were several of them.

They had been used in his father's time as well as warming pans to heat the beds at night.

He put the bottle on top of the stove to warm it, and looked in the other cupboards.

He was hoping he would find some chocolate or anything similar to make a hot drink.

One of his relations had come to stay with him a short while ago.

He had the idea she had brought her own chocolate, to which she was very partial, with her.

He was not mistaken.

He found the pot and he reckoned there was just enough chocolate left for Safina.

It all took time.

Finally he went back upstairs, carrying the

hot-water bottle, a cup of chocolate, and his candle.

He was half afraid that Safina would have regained consciousness and perhaps had run away again.

It was with a sense of relief that he entered her bedroom and found her still in bed.

He put the chocolate and the candle down on the table beside her.

Lifting the blankets where her feet were, he put the hot-water bottle near them.

As he did so, he touched one foot and found, as he had expected, it was very cold.

He was tucking the blanket under the mattress again when Safina stirred.

She opened her eyes, and as she did so she gave a little cry.

It was hardly audible, but the Duke bent over her to say gently:

"It is all right, you are quite safe."

She stared at him, and then she said in a slightly clearer tone:

"What . . . what . . . has . . . happened?"

He sat down on the mattress facing her, and taking her hand, held it in both of his to warm it.

"Everything is all right," he said, "you are in your own bed and no-one will hurt you."

For a moment she did not understand.

Then gradually the memory of what she had done came back to her.

He saw the colour rise in her cheeks.

"I ... I drowned ... myself," she said in a whisper.

"You tried to," the Duke corrected her, "and it was a very wrong and wicked thing to do."

His fingers tightened for a moment on hers as he said:

"Why did you not tell me you were frightened of me?"

Her eyes flickered and the colour deepened in her cheeks.

"It was all my fault," the Duke said, "and now I have a suggestion to make. Are you listening to me, Safina?"

She had turned her head to one side, but her eyes were still open and she answered faintly:

"I ... am ... listening."

"As I have said," the Duke went on, "it was my fault for not realising how young you are and how deeply you were upset by your Stepmother and everything that has happened today."

He paused before continuing:

"So I am asking you to forgive me, Safina. Please let us start again in a very different manner."

He felt her fingers quiver in his.

He knew that she was still apprehensive and perhaps as fearful as she had been when she had run away.

"What we were trying to do," the Duke said, "or, rather, I was, was to start in the middle of a story instead of at the beginning."

She made a little murmur, but he was not certain if she understood.

"What I am suggesting," he went on, "and I hope you will agree, is that we begin at Chapter One—when we first met."

He was speaking in this way because he knew how intelligent she was.

He thought it would appeal to her imagination.

She had already told him when they visited the Library how thrilled she was to see so many books.

"Do . . . you mean . . ." Safina started to say, and then was too embarrassed to go any further.

"What I mean," the Duke said firmly, "is that we get to know each other. We have met today and we are like two people castaway on a Desert Island who have never met each other before and have to use their wits to save themselves from extinction."

Slowly Safina turned her head back so that she could look at him directly.

"That is exactly what has . . . happened," she whispered.

"Of course it is," the Duke said, "and this house is indeed a kind of Desert Island, only lacking the wild bananas we could eat to keep ourselves alive and the fish we could cook if we were clever enough to catch them."

Safina gave a weak little chuckle.

"You are . . . making it . . . into a . . . story."

"It *is* a story, if you think about it," the Duke answered, "and as we have to be the hero and heroine in it, we must not do anything which will spoil the readers' enjoyment of our adventure."

His fingers tightened a little on hers as he said:

"Promise you will not run away again and leave me all alone. Even Robinson Crusoe eventually had Man Friday with him."

Now Safina gave what was almost a weak laugh.

"That is . . . not very . . . complimentary."

"In our story," the Duke replied, "the heroine found a stranger who was ship-wrecked with her. He was an understanding and intelligent man who was prepared to do *anything* she asked of him."

As he spoke, his eyes met Safina's and they looked at each other in the light of the candle.

"I am . . . sorry," she whispered. "It was . . . stupid of . . . me to be so . . . frightened."

"I understand," the Duke said, "and you must promise to forgive me for my stupidity."

"And . . . now," Safina said in a very small voice, "we are . . . friends."

"Friends," the Duke replied, "or, rather, shall we say partners? If we survive, we have to share everything that is at our disposal."

Safina gave an exclamation, and then she said:

"I had an . . . idea when . . . we came back . . .

to the house after . . . looking at . . . the lake."

She paused and murmured:

"I know it was very . . . wrong of me to . . . try to . . . drown myself . . . Papa would have been . . . ashamed of my . . . being such a . . . coward."

"You are not to think of it again," the Duke said. "No-one will ever know it happened and you and I will forget it."

"Can . . . you really do . . . that?"

"I have forgotten it already," he answered.

As if she suddenly thought of it, Safina said:

"You . . . must have . . . carried me back . . . and undressed . . . me."

The colour was back again to her cheeks, and the Duke said:

"You are not to think about it, and you were not very heavy."

"I . . . made you . . . wet too."

"I was soaked," the Duke said. "I will tell Banks I have been swimming and as I look after my own clothes, I will dry them in front of the fire."

He remembered as he spoke he had left his night-shirt by the lake.

He told himself he must remember to fetch it before the morning.

"Now," he said, "all that is forgotten, and you were going to tell me something."

"I have thought of two things," Safina said, "but you may think . . . them rather . . . foolish."

"If I do, I will say so," the Duke replied.

"But so far since we have been on our Desert Island, you have not said anything foolish."

Safina was silent for a moment, but he saw there was a light in her eyes that had not been there before.

"I remembered," she began, "when that woman Mrs. Hewins was asking for the leaves from the Magic Tree, that when I was in Florence, once a year the Nuns celebrated the anniversary of the Founder of the Convent."

She looked at the Duke to see if he was listening and went on:

"Her name was Costanza, and there is a Saint of that name."

"I expect I have heard of her," the Duke said.

"What the Nuns did," Safina continued, "was to take tiny pieces from the habit of the Founder of the Convent and encase them in little nickel frames and they were supposed to give those who possessed them a Blessing all through the following year."

The Duke made a little murmur, as if he realised where the story was leading, but he did not interrupt.

"One of these sacred emblems," Safina continued, "was dipped in gold and sent to His Holiness the Pope."

"Do you really think we could do that with the leaves from King Charles' Tree?" the Duke enquired.

"Why not?" Safina asked. "If they are so lucky for the people in the village, if they knew about them, people from all over England would want them too."

"It is certainly an idea," the Duke answered.

He remembered as he spoke that many of the members of Whites Club, however cynical they might pretend to be about such things, believed in lucky charms and omens.

He knew there were quite a number who would not make a bet on Friday the thirteenth.

One member carried a hare's foot which was traditionally supposed to be lucky.

Another treasured a rhinoceros horn which he had brought back with him from Africa.

There were a dozen or more who had different superstitions they observed.

Although he himself had laughed at such things, he had often longed for an omen that things would get better in the future.

"Perhaps you are right," he said aloud, "but I cannot believe we would make enough money from that to do any great repairs on the house."

"I have not told . . . you my . . . second . . . idea," Safina said.

"I am listening," the Duke answered.

"It is not quite clear in my mind, and I meant to think it out . . . tonight when I . . . went to . . . bed."

She gave him a quick glance.

He knew she was remembering how she had run away and thought in the morning she would not be there.

"You are breaking your promise," he said sternly.

She gave him a shy little smile and went on:

"You may . . . think this is . . . impossible, but I am . . . sure we can . . . do it."

"Do what?" the Duke asked.

"First we have somehow to borrow money on the thirty thousand pounds I come into when I am twenty-five, and also on the fortune I shall receive when Papa dies."

She was aware the Duke stiffened, and she said quickly:

"We will not go to Usurers, who, I have read, are very grasping and extort huge sums from their clients."

She paused before continuing:

"But I think that our Solicitors could talk to a Bank, and as you are a Duke, they cannot say you are not respectable."

The Duke laughed.

"There is no guarantee of that. But if we get the money, what do you propose to do with it?"

"That is what we shall have to explain to who-ever lends it to us."

She drew in her breath before she said:

"We restore the house and make it magnificent as it was before. Then we let people pay to come to see it."

The Duke stared at her.

"I had the idea," she said hastily before he could speak, "when I remembered there was an Italian Prince who lived near Florence who had

110

the most splendid collection of pictures."

She moved a little higher up on her pillow, as it was easier to talk when she was not lying so flat.

"He could not bear to sell any of them, but as he was very poor, he thought he would be obliged to do so."

"He was lucky he had something to sell," the Duke remarked.

"He loved his pictures and was determined not to do so," Safina continued.

"So what did he do?" the Duke asked.

"He opened his Picture Gallery and other rooms in his house as if they were a museum."

"You mean people paid to view them?"

"The pictures were famous, and hundreds if not thousands of people went to his Palazzo every year so that eventually he was able to close his doors again and have them all to himself."

There was silence for a moment, and then the Duke said:

"Are you seriously suggesting that that is what we might do?"

"Why not?" Safina answered. "You know as well as I do that ordinary people as well as tourists would love to see inside a Ducal Mansion."

She saw by the Duke's expression that he was thinking that it would be unpleasant to have outsiders tramping around his house.

"I am convinced," she said, "that we shall make so much money in perhaps no more than five years that you will be able to pay back your debts and then have the house all to yourself."

"All to *ourselves*," the Duke corrected her. "It is certainly an idea."

He spoke slowly, as if he were beginning to think it out, and Safina said:

"We will have to show the visitors around, and we will need to have guides if we are not there. Of course they must be men we can trust to make sure that nobody steals anything."

"I think perhaps a number of my friends and neighbours would be shocked at my going into trade in such a very strange way," the Duke remarked.

"They would be much more shocked if you die of starvation," Safina retorted. "I do not suppose any of them have offered to help you out of your difficulties by writing a cheque."

"I have no wish to accept charity," the Duke said coldly.

Safina laughed.

"Now you are being proud! Personally I would accept anything from anyone rather than go hungry!"

She paused before adding:

"And you should think of the feelings of your house rather than of yourself."

The Duke's eyes twinkled as she went on:

"Of course the poor thing minds looking so shabby and down-at-heel. I am quite certain that it has feelings of its own and resents every moment that there is water dripping down its face and holes in the windows that let in the wind."

The Duke laughed.

"I think we must explore what you have suggested, Safina, and now you must go to sleep."

"Is that . . . all you have to . . . say about . . . my idea?"

"No," he replied. "I think it is original, brilliant, and far cleverer than anything I should ever have expected from a young woman."

"Now you are being pompous and patronising," Safina protested. "If you want the truth, I think because I was standing under your Magic Tree when I thought about it that once again it has proved itself lucky."

"Very well," the Duke said, "you have convinced me and we will talk about it tomorrow."

"Tomorrow!" Safina cried. "That has given me another idea."

"What is it now?" he asked.

"We need food, and I suppose somebody must go to the village to collect it."

"I will do that," the Duke said.

"Then I suggest," Safina said, "if it is possible, that you send a carriage to collect the Solicitor who looks after my and Papa's affairs. His main office is in Canterbury which is, I think, not far from here and only ten miles from Wick Park."

"I think I can beg, borrow, or hire a carriage," the Duke said slowly.

"Then send for Mr. Metcalfe immediately. The

firm is Metcalfe, Metcalfe, and Storton, and their address is easy: Number One, The High Street."

The Duke smiled.

"I will obey your orders."

"If you are going to be snooty about everything," Safina said, "I shall run away again."

"If you do that," the Duke answered, "I shall let the fish eat you, or give you a good smacking, which is obviously something you omitted to experience when you were a naughty child."

Safina laughed, and then the Duke was laughing too.

"Is this really happening?" she asked. "I think actually I must have . . . drowned and am now . . . dreaming."

"You are being very sensible and very practical," the Duke said, "and I am really very grateful. But I am beginning to think that my partner on the Desert Island is a somewhat bossy young woman."

"And I am thinking that the old Fuddy-Duddy with whom I am marooned should have thought of these things for himself."

Then they were both laughing again and the Duke rose to his feet.

"I am going to bed," he said, "and make no mistake: By the morning this Fuddy-Duddy will have some new ideas and a great many orders for his partner. She might start, for instance, by dusting the house."

"Now you are being spiteful," Safina protested.

"You have already agreed that we shall have some more servants, young ones to help that poor old couple downstairs. You can engage those when you are in the village as well as getting the food."

The Duke clicked his heels together and saluted.

"Very good, General," he said. "I will do my best."

Safina laughed.

"I will doubtless sleep late," she said, "so you had better take the money I have in my bag in case the shops will not give you credit."

"If you say any more," the Duke replied, "you will get that spanking I have already promised you!"

"Stop being proud because I am a woman," Safina retorted. "You know as well as I do that you would be embarrassed to ask for more credit and they will be delighted to take any money you have available. If I were a man, you would not hesitate."

"But you are not," the Duke replied.

It flashed through his mind how very beautiful she looked when he dried her.

After all, she was his wife!

He wondered what she would say if he suggested that he kiss her to seal their partnership.

Then he was afraid that once again she would be terrified of him and run away when she knew he was asleep.

"Where is this money?" he asked.

"My bag is in the right-hand drawer of the dressing-table."

He walked towards it and opened her hand-bag which, he realised, was a very expensive one and had doubtless been bought in Florence.

He was surprised to find that inside there were a number of sovereigns and several notes of large value.

He looked at them enquiringly, and Safina explained:

"I changed all the Italian money I had before I left Florence at the bank. They were very obliging and so I also cashed a cheque, thinking I might have a lot of things to buy as soon as I reached London."

She thought for a moment, as she spoke, of her Stepmother, how she had arranged for her to be taken from Dover to the Posting Inn.

Then she thrust the memory aside.

"Take all that is there," she said, "for food and wages, and as I did not spend all my allowance when I was at School I have quite a considerable sum in the Bank."

She laughed before she went on:

"Not enough to repair the house, but at least to make you and me as partners more comfortable than we are at the moment."

She emphasised the word *partners*.

As the Duke reluctantly took the money from her bag as she had told him to do, he said almost beneath his breath:

"Partners, I must keep remembering that is what we are."

"And as you have said yourself," Safina replied as if she must have the last word, "there are no bananas growing on this Desert Island and therefore you have to buy them."

chapter six

SAFINA looked around the Study and thought it looked better.

She had got up early to find to her surprise that the Duke had already left for the village.

She had her tea alone.

Then she went into the garden to pick lilac both white and purple, tulips, and daffodils.

She arranged them in a number of vases and put them on the furniture.

Then she searched in the other rooms to find cushions that were not faded and torn for the chairs.

Although she thought the Duke would laugh at her, she found a large piece of embroidery.

She used it to cover the back of the sofa which was so torn that the stuffing showed.

She had herself re-lit the fire, but had not removed the ashes from the night before.

There was no shovel or bucket available for that.

Now the room looked quite different from what it had, and she hoped the Duke would appreciate it.

The curtains needed washing and the furniture polishing.

She dusted what she could.

When the sun came through the windows she thought as a Sitting-Room it was at least passable.

She had just finished arranging the last vase, which was a small one, when she thought she heard the Duke return.

She had put in it the first rose-buds that peeped their way through the weeds in what had been the Rose Garden.

She placed the vase on the Duke's desk and hoped he would be pleased when he saw it.

When he came into the room, she looked up eagerly.

"Good morning, Safina," he said. "When I left you, you were snoring happily."

"I do not snore," Safina retorted, then realised he was teasing her.

"I was told you had gone to the village," she said.

"I have carried out all your orders, Senior Partner," he replied.

"All of them?" Safina enquired.

"There are three servants arriving later in the day—a footman for the hall, a competent young woman to work in the Kitchen, and another to look after you, and, of course, obey your orders."

"Just three?" Safina questioned.

"That is enough to begin with," the Duke answered, "but I did ask Mr. Geary to find me two women who would come up every morning to gradually clean the whole house."

Safina laughed.

"Poor things, that is certainly a Herculean task! And who is Mr. Geary?"

"The most important man in the village," the Duke replied. "He owns the only shop which is also a Post-Office, and his brother, who is next door, is the Butcher."

The Duke smiled before he added:

"He nearly had a stroke when I gave him twenty pounds of your money, but I still owe him quite a lot more."

"And Mr. Metcalfe?" Safina asked.

"Carrying out your instructions," the Duke said. "I sent a carriage to collect him, and I reckon he should be here early in the afternoon."

"That is splendid," Safina said, "and I suppose you told him why he was wanted?"

"I asked him to come here as soon as he possibly could since you need to see him urgently. I did not tell him we were married, as I thought it would be too much of a shock."

"I am sure it will be," Safina said, "and I suppose we had better be frank about the whole thing."

She paused before adding:

"Papa has always said one should not lie to one's Solicitor or one's Doctor."

"Your father is right," the Duke answered. "At the same time, it is a mistake for more people to know about us than is absolutely necessary."

"I agree with that," Safina answered.

The Duke looked around the Study.

"You have waved a magic wand," he said. "I am sure Mr. Metcalfe will be impressed."

"I did it for you," Safina said, "so that you would not . . . feel so gloomy or . . . so disagreeable."

Now she was teasing him, and the Duke said:

"What woman could refuse such a challenge? I mean, of course, to make a home on a Desert Island."

"It really does look better," Safina said.

"Very much better," the Duke agreed, "and I have never thought of picking flowers for myself."

"There are not only flowers in the vases," Safina said. "What else do you see there?"

The Duke looked closely at the big case filled with white and purple lilac and quite a number of leaves.

He stared at them for a moment, and then he exclaimed:

"Of course, the Magic Tree!"

"Exactly," Safina said, "and since I am prepared to believe in it even if you are not, I am wearing some leaves here."

She touched the front of her chest, just between her breasts.

The Duke remembered how exquisite they had looked when he undressed her last night.

Because he thought he was treading on forbidden ground, he said quickly:

"If I do have some luck, I shall believe it is you and not the tree that has made the change."

"I hope that is true," Safina replied. "There is another thing you have forgotten to tell me."

"What is that?" the Duke asked.

"If you have ordered any food."

"I have ordered enough to delight Mr. Geary. He is sending it all up in his cart, with the young woman he has chosen to help Mrs. Banks, who he assures me is the best cook in the village."

Safina clapped her hands together.

"Now things are really looking up."

"Thanks to you," the Duke said.

"Thanks, I believe, to the Magic Tree," Safina replied, "so if you must say who is responsible for what, that is really thanks to you."

"I am perfectly prepared to accept the congratulations when the good luck occurs."

"You will do that after we have seen Mr. Metcalfe," Safina said optimistically.

She knew, the Duke thought, although he did not say so, that she was raising her hopes too high.

Later in the afternoon Mr. Metcalfe was driven away in the same carriage which had brought him to Wyn Park.

Safina slipped her hand into the Duke's as they waved goodbye at the front-door and said:

"I told you the leaves were magic."

"I believe every word that has ever been said about them," the Duke replied.

The meeting with Mr. Metcalfe had certainly been encouraging.

When after he had greeted Safina and she told him she was married, he was astounded.

"I understood," he said, "from your father, Lady Safina, whom I saw only a week ago, that you were returning from Florence to take part in the Season and to make your curtsy at Buckingham Palace."

Safina glanced at the Duke.

To save her embarrassment, he said:

"We are going to tell you the truth of what has happened, Mr. Metcalfe, and I feel sure when you hear what we have to say, you will agree that it must remain a secret from everyone else except yourself."

He then proceeded to tell the Solicitor how the Countess had written to the Convent to have Safina brought back to England while her father was away.

He related how she had been met at Dover by Mr. Carter and taken to an obscure Posting House.

From there she was conveyed to Wyn Park,

where she was married to him the moment she arrived.

"You mean, Your Grace, you had never met each other before?" Mr. Metcalfe asked.

"We had never ever seen each other," the Duke answered, "and the Countess threatened Lady Safina that if she did not agree to marry me, she would be placed in a Lunatic Asylum and no-one might ever know where she was."

Mr. Metcalfe stared at him, incredulous.

"I can hardly believe what you are telling me, Your Grace."

"We can hardly believe it ourselves," the Duke replied. "I need not go into details, but I, for my part, had to submit to the Countess's blackmail because a Lady's reputation was involved."

He did not need to say any more.

He knew by the expression in Mr. Metcalfe's eyes that he had a very clear idea of the situation.

"Now that I am married," Safina chimed in, "you will understand, Mr. Metcalfe, I wish to help His Grace to restore his house and free him from a multitude of debts which he has no means of meeting."

Mr. Metcalfe smiled and replied:

"That should not be difficult, Your Grace. I am sure your father—"

Safina put up her hand.

"There is something else we have not told you, which is that my Stepmother has made it clear that she will not allow my father to give me one penny of the fortune he inherited from my mother."

Mr. Metcalfe looked horrified.

"As she is so young," Safina went on, "she is determined to get everything possible into her own hands before my father dies, when, as you are well aware, my mother's money becomes mine."

"But surely . . ." Mr. Metcalfe began.

"It is no use," Safina said. "Papa gives in to her because he is besotted by her, and she is determined to prevent me from having any more than I possess already."

"That I know," Mr. Metcalfe said, "is the thirty thousand pounds your mother left you, but you cannot touch the capital until you are twenty-five."

"Exactly," Safina said, "and that is what I have told His Grace. But I have an idea and that is where we need your help."

She then told him how she planned to restore the house and make it as beautiful as it had been in the past, how she was sure they could attract a large influx of visitors who would pay for the privilege of going round it.

Mr. Metcalfe was astonished, but he did not speak, and Safina went on:

"I also want to sell leaves from His Grace's Magic Tree which was planted by King Charles II."

"I have heard of that tree," Mr. Metcalfe exclaimed.

"You have?" the Duke asked in surprise.

"One of my friends who was passing Wyn Park once was daring enough to go up the drive and look at your house from the outside."

He paused before continuing:

"He had been told in the Inn where he had luncheon about Your Grace's Tree, and as there seemed to be no-one about, he helped himself to several leaves which he was convinced brought him a great deal of unexpected luck."

Safina gave a cry of delight.

"There you are!" she said to the Duke. "I know if we made little cachets of them to sell, we would make a fortune."

"I am prepared to believe everything," the Duke said, "but I have the uncomfortable feeling that any money we obtain from the Tree will be fairy gold."

"Nonsense," Safina said, "it will be good solid gold which Mr. Metcalfe will invest for us."

The Duke laughed, and Mr. Metcalfe said:

"It may be difficult to raise a loan as substantial as you require, Your Grace. At the same time, even the Banks and the Money-Lenders are influenced by the social status of their clients. Therefore I am hopeful I shall be able to do something for you."

"Do you really mean that?" Safina exclaimed. "Oh, Mr. Metcalfe, I knew you would not fail me!"

"It may not be a large enough loan to do everything you require," Mr. Metcalfe said, "but at least if you begin by restoring a few rooms in the house, say the Picture Gallery, the Ball Room, the Library, and perhaps one of the State Bedrooms, it would be enough to attract the sightseers, whether they are English or foreigners."

Safina clasped her hands together.

"It sounds too wonderful," she said, "and if it seems to be a success, do you mean we could extend the loan and of course save every penny we can to restore more and more rooms?"

"That is what I advise," Mr. Metcalfe said.

He looked at the Duke as he spoke, who said:

"I can hardly believe what I am hearing! After being in the depths of despair for so long, it is difficult to believe the sun is shining."

"I will be frank with Your Grace," Mr. Metcalfe said. "It would not be at all easy if people were not aware of the enormous fortune Her Grace will inherit eventually."

He paused before adding somewhat sarcastically:

"Even the Countess, extravagant though she is, could not manage to make any really deep inroads into the capital sum which is continually increasing."

"I had no idea that this was general knowledge," the Duke said somewhat stiffly.

"People talk, Your Grace," Mr. Metcalfe said, "and whilst the Earl is very reticent on the subject, there is no-one who in one way or another is not interested in money even if it belongs to someone else."

The Duke had to laugh.

"That is true," he answered.

He rose from the chair in which he was sitting and said:

"Now, as you have cheered us up and made the future seem very much brighter than it has ever been before, I am going to fetch you some refreshment."

"I am sure Banks or the footman will do that," Safina said, "if you ring the bell."

The Duke looked at her, and then he laughed.

"I had forgotten we had a footman," he said, "and as I bought a bottle of Champagne in the village and carried it home myself, I was not expecting to be waited on."

"You will soon get used to the idea," Safina said as she smiled.

The Duke rang the bell.

It was answered by Banks bringing in a bottle of Claret on a tray with three glasses.

He set it down on a side-table and poured out the wine.

He handed it first to Safina, then to Mr. Metcalfe, and lastly the Duke.

As he did so, Safina thought that now that he had help and a new era was starting in the house, Banks really looked younger.

She also thought the good food they had eaten last night and what they had enjoyed at Luncheon was already making a difference.

She was quite sure it was also affecting the Duke.

He had certainly been much more cheerful and very charming to her all through the meal.

'Thank You, thank You,' she said in her heart, and it was a prayer.

Because she was also grateful to the Magic Tree, she touched the leaves she could feel against her skin.

As she did so, she caught the Duke's eyes and was aware he knew what she was doing.

There was an expression in his eyes which made her suddenly feel shy, and she blushed.

Mr. Metcalfe sipped the Claret, and after he had drunk a little he said:

"When I received your message, Your Grace, it seemed strange that you should want me so urgently, and I thought perhaps you were in need of money."

He paused before continuing:

"I therefore brought with me just in case you needed it a hundred pounds in cash."

Safina gave a cry of delight.

"Of course I want it, and it was very clever of you, Mr. Metcalfe, to guess how necessary it is."

She looked at the Duke and added:

"That will pay the bills in the village, but I think you should ask Mr. Metcalfe to do something about the pensioners, and of course give him all your other bills which must be paid as soon as we have the loan."

She saw the Duke's lips tighten and thought he was going to be difficult.

She therefore added quickly;

"You have not explained to Mr. Metcalfe that we have gone into Partnership over this matter. You supply the house, the pictures, and all the other wonderful treasures there are here, while for the moment I find the money. Later our positions may easily be reversed."

"I think that is unlikely," the Duke said, "but at the same time, Mr. Metcalfe, I would be extremely grateful if you could carry out my wife's wishes."

"Leave everything to me," Mr. Metcalfe said. "My Partners and I have many other important Clients as well as the Earl of Sedgewick, and it is difficult for any Bank to refuse us what we want."

He rose to his feet and put his empty glass down on the table.

"Now, if you will excuse me," he said, "I will go back to my office and start immediately on the task you have set me."

Safina was so excited that she felt like flinging her arms around the Solicitor and kissing him.

She had known him since she was a child and he was a very well preserved fifty-five years old.

Instead, she said:

"Thank you, thank you! My husband I can never be grateful enough for your encouragement and your promise of help. Please let it be soon."

"I shall go to London tomorrow," Mr. Metcalfe

assured her, "and I hope that I shall have good news within three or four days."

Safina looked at the Duke, and her eyes were shining like stars.

Although for the moment he did not say anything, she thought that a burden had fallen from his shoulders.

She was sure he was as thrilled as she was.

They said goodbye to Mr. Metcalfe and watched the carriage which was taking him away until it vanished among the trees on the drive.

"We have won!" Safina exclaimed. "Do you realise we have won a tremendous battle?"

"It was our Waterloo," the Duke said, "and you were Wellington!"

"He would not have been very much use without his troops and his cannons behind him. That, my dear Partner, is Wyn Park, which belongs to you."

"You have an answer for everything," the Duke smiled.

They walked back to the Study and he poured himself another glass of Claret.

Safina's glass was still half-full.

"I am quite sure I am dreaming," he said.

"Then we must be very careful not to wake up," Safina replied, "and as I refuse to wait for 'the off,' I suggest we ride into the village and find what workmen there are to start on the house immediately, beginning, as Mr. Metcalfe suggested, with the Picture Gallery."

"Very well," the Duke said, "but I think the hall must come first, and the outside. Otherwise your sight-seers will begrudge paying an entrance fee before they reach the Picture Gallery."

"Of course you are right," Safina agreed. "Oh, do get the horses and let us make sure the workmen are here first thing tomorrow morning."

The Duke laughed.

Because she was so enthusiastic and eager and it was actually what he wanted himself, he agreed.

He had not changed from his riding clothes, so he did as Safina suggested and went towards the Stables.

He wondered if it would be too much for the horse he had already ridden to go out again.

Then he remembered that he had ordered Mr. Geary to send up several bags of the very best oats, the sort he had never been able to afford before.

He was not surprised when he reached the Stables to find that both horses had been fed.

He knew that Banks had a soft spot for all animals, and he had known how much the oats were wanted.

"I will get Mr. Geary to find me a Stable boy," the Duke told himself.

He lifted down a bridle and carried it into the first stall.

He was still finding it hard to believe that what Safina had suggested was possible, and that Metcalfe, who, he realised, was an extremely intelligent and respected Solicitor, had agreed.

'If Isobel thought she was making me more unhappy than I was already,' the Duke thought, 'she is going to be disappointed.'

He saddled the horses.

Then he found himself thinking, as he had last night, of Safina's beauty.

How different she was from any other woman he had known before!

She appeared this morning to have forgotten the terror which had made her try to drown herself.

He could not imagine any of the women to whom he had made love getting up so early.

They would not have made the Study look so different from what it had when he was alone.

And they would certainly have been incapable of explaining the situation so clearly and sensibly to Mr. Metcalfe.

"She is extraordinary," he told himself. "So unexpectedly clever and yet in some ways so child-like."

He thought it was very touching that she had put the leaves from the Magic Tree between her breasts.

Yet her faith in them had been justified.

"She has certainly brought me luck," he told himself.

He rode one horse and led the other round to the front of the building.

He had just reached the steps leading up to

the front-door when Safina came running down them.

She looked very lovely in a smart riding-habit that had been made for her in Florence.

She had one of the small, fashionable riding-hats on her head.

It had a gauze veil around the crown which hung down behind.

The Duke dismounted so he could lift her into the saddle.

He put his hands around her waist.

As he did so, he remembered how small it had seemed last night when he had dried it and how beautiful her body was.

Then he was aware she was looking at him and reading his thoughts.

The colour rose in her cheeks.

As he paused before lifting her up, they were close to each other.

Her lips were near his.

The Duke suddenly wanted to kiss her.

He felt the blood throbbing in his temples at the thought of how soft her lips would be.

Then he told himself it was much too soon, and he might easily frighten her again.

Quickly he swung her up on the saddle.

As she took up her reins he adjusted her skirt over the stirrups.

As he walked to his own horse, he knew, though it seemed impossible, that he had not thought of Yvonne de Mauzon since he had been married to Safina.

She was moving away down the drive.

As he followed her, he thought again it seemed impossible.

Yet nothing could be more fascinating than what was happening to him at this moment.

"I have to make her trust me," he told himself.

That was more important than anything else.

chapter seven

"IT has been an exciting day," the Duke said as they went up the stairs.

"It has been wonderful, absolutely wonderful," Safina answered, "and I can still hardly believe that the workmen would find the original panelling in the hall, under all that paper and paint."

It was just one of the discoveries that had been made in the last two days.

They had received a letter from Mr. Metcalfe saying that he had obtained for them a loan of twenty thousand pounds.

Safina had jumped about with joy.

The Duke knew that he had only to ride into the village and tell Mr. Geary to send a number of other workmen up to the house next morning.

He thought that every carpenter, painter, and gilder in the whole county would now be working at Wyn.

There was so much to do—planning the rooms, supervising those that had just started, and choosing paint for the others.

In fact, he and Safina hardly had time to speak to each other during the day.

It was only when the workmen had gone home and they dined in whatever room had not been emptied of furniture that they could talk.

Dinner that evening had been in what had once been a small breakfast-room.

"I have finished the first two leaf cachets today," Safina said, "which I intend to dip in gold. The first is for you and the second for Mr. Metcalfe."

The Duke smiled.

"I really do not need one when I have you."

"Of course you need one," Safina replied, "and it is entirely due to the wonderful Magic Tree that all these exciting things have happened."

The Duke knew that that was what she believed with all her heart.

He was convinced personally that it was she who had brought him luck.

He was wondering how he could tell her how much she meant to him.

Because she was so unselfconscious and was thinking only of the house and what they were doing to it, she had no idea what the Duke was feeling about her.

Every day, every hour, every minute, he found himself being more and more attracted by her.

"I am falling in love," he told himself, "and it is different from anything I have ever felt before for anyone."

Yet he was still afraid to tell her so.

He might shatter what he knew for her was an idealistic friendship which she had never had with any other man.

"Suppose she is frightened and hates me again?" he asked in the darkness of the night.

Thinking of Safina made him toss restlessly in his bed.

He found it impossible to sleep.

She was in the next room, and he had only to open the two communicating-doors to be with her.

He could feel his desire for her burning inside him.

Then he remembered how she had looked when he had lifted her unconscious from the waters of the lake.

He had thought for a moment that she had actually drowned.

When he carried her back to the house he had wondered what he would do if she never came back to life.

He had imagined all too vividly the scandal it would cause.

Someone was bound to find out that she had drowned herself after they had been forcibly married by Isobel.

Yet now, incredibly, he knew it was the luckiest thing that had ever happened to him.

Not because Safina had brought him money, that was incidental, but because she had taken a place in his house and in his heart that had always been empty.

He had been intrigued, attracted, fascinated, and even infatuated by quite a number of women.

But what he felt about Safina was very different.

He could hardly explain it to himself.

First of all, he felt an urge to look after her, to protect her from her Stepmother and from anyone else who might frighten or upset her.

Then, because she was so beautiful, he desired her; of course he did.

Yet it was very different from the fiery, burning desire which would shoot violently into flames and die down just as quickly.

"This is real love," he had told himself last night.

He had been standing in his bedroom, looking up at the stars in the sky overhead.

Now, as they reached Safina's bedroom door, the Duke said;

"I think you will sleep well tonight."

"I expect so," Safina replied. "At the same time, I hate wasting the hours when we might be working."

The Duke laughed.

"If you drive the workmen any harder," he

said, "they will undoubtedly go on strike."

"Then we will have to do it all ourselves," Safina retorted.

"God forbid!" the Duke exclaimed in horror, holding up his hands.

Safina laughed and went into her bedroom.

"Goodnight," she said, and shut the door.

The Duke stood for a moment without moving.

He was wondering, if he had put his arms around her and kissed her goodnight, what she would have said.

Then with a sigh he walked the short distance to his own door and went in.

For a long time he stood as he had the previous evening, looking at the stars.

Then, as they reminded him of Safina's eyes, he forced himself to undress and get into bed.

'Tomorrow,' he thought, 'perhaps there will be an opportunity for me to tell her how much she means to me.'

Then he told himself it was no use thinking about Safina or he would have another sleepless night.

He was about to blow out the candles beside his bed when he realised he had not read a newspaper for two days.

It was impossible to put anything down in the rooms on the ground floor which were all being renovated.

Banks had therefore laid *The Times* on a chair by his bed.

The Duke reached out and, opening it, started to look at the headlines.

Because he and Safina talked and thought only of the house, the events of the world outside seemed remote and unimportant.

He turned over the pages and forced himself to read the Editorial.

He was half-way through it when there was a sound of a door opening.

The Duke looked up and saw to his astonishment Safina come into the room.

She was wearing only her thin night-gown, and her hair was falling over her shoulders.

He was so surprised at her appearance that for a moment he could only stare at her.

He thought she could not be real, but a vision that he was seeing in his mind.

Then she said in a voice he could hardly hear:

"I am . . . frightened."

"Frightened?" the Duke exclaimed. "What has happened?"

He sat up, flinging the paper down on the floor beside him.

"It . . . is . . . Stepmama," Safina answered.

Then she gave a little cry.

"She is . . . cursing us . . . it . . . is . . . horrible!"

Now there was the frantic note the Duke had heard in her voice before.

She suddenly ran across the room and flung herself against him.

His arms went around her and she hid her face against his shoulder.

Almost incoherently she stammered:

"There . . . was a . . . b-bat in . . . my . . . room . . . when I . . . awoke . . . I thought . . . S-Step-mama was th-there too . . . I could . . . h-hear her . . . c-cursing me . . . Sh-she will . . . t-try to . . . t-take me . . . a-away. S-stop her . . . Oh . . . stop . . . her."

The Duke's arms tightened.

"No-one will take you away," he said. "You are mine, Safina, and your Stepmother cannot hurt you any more."

"She . . . is . . . wicked . . . she is . . . evil . . . she is . . . putting a . . . spell on . . . me."

Safina raised her head.

The Duke saw in the candle-light the terror in her eyes and the tears running down her cheeks.

"Save . . . me . . . save . . . me," she whispered frantically.

For a moment he just looked at her, thinking he had never seen anyone look more lovely.

Then he drew her close him and his lips were on hers.

He felt her stiffen with surprise before her body seemed to melt into his.

He pulled her closer still and laid her down on the pillow.

Then, as he kissed her and went on kissing her, he felt the ecstasy he was giving her rise within himself.

Nothing mattered, except that they were part of each other and Safina was his.

He kissed her until he knew she was no longer frightened.

He raised his head and looked down at her.

In the candle-light he could see her face was radiant with an almost unhuman beauty that transformed her.

For a moment he just looked at her.

Then he was kissing her again, kissing her with possessive, demanding, and passionate kisses.

They told her without words how much he wanted her.

It was not only the softness and sweetness of her lips which excited him, but her body close against his.

His kisses were lifting her up into the sky towards the stars.

Neither of them were on earth, but outside the gates of Heaven.

In a voice that was very unsteady and unlike his own the Duke said:

"I love you, my precious, I love you and I want you completely and absolutely as my wife."

"I love . . . you," Safina murmured, "but I . . . did not . . . know it was . . . love."

"But you do love me," the Duke insisted.

"There is . . . nothing else but . . . you in the . . . whole world," Safina replied. "You are . . . the sky . . . the moon and . . . the stars. I never knew . . . before that I . . . could touch . . . them."

There was a dream-like ecstasy in her voice.

Then he was kissing her again, kissing her until she said:

"You will . . . not let . . . anyone take . . . me away from . . . you."

He knew she was thinking of her Stepmother, and he said fiercely:

"I will kill anybody who tries to take you from me. You are mine, Safina, mine and, my darling, I want you, I want you now at this very moment."

He knew she did not completely understand, but she said in the child-like voice he loved:

"I . . . am yours . . . all yours and . . . please hold me very . . . tight so I am . . . no longer . . . afraid."

It was then something broke within the Duke and he kissed her wildly, passionately, demandingly, almost as if he were fighting away the enemies that would take her from him.

He kissed her eyes, her lips, her neck, her breasts.

Safina was not afraid.

Something wild and wonderful leapt within her.

She felt the fire burning on his lips and she was aware there were tiny flames flickering within her breasts.

It was wonderful, absolutely perfect.

Something which she had known vaguely was there, if only she could find it, now at last was hers.

Then, as the Duke made her his, they passed

through the gates of Heaven and were part of the Divine.

* * *

A long time later, Safina stirred against the Duke's shoulder.

"Are you awake, my darling?" he asked.

"I think I am . . . dreaming and it is so . . . wonderful, so perfect . . . I am . . . afraid of . . . waking up."

His arms tightened as he said:

"That is how I feel too. Do you still love me?"

"I love . . . you until . . . there is . . . only love and . . . you!"

"That is what I feel," the Duke said. "How is it possible that we have found each other? Whatever happens, we are together for eternity."

"Are you . . . sure of . . . that?" Safina whispered.

"Absolutely sure," he replied, "and that I am incredibly lucky to possess anything so beautiful and so perfect in every way."

His hand was running over her body as he spoke.

As he felt her quiver, he said:

"If you only knew how much you have tortured me because I was so afraid that you would never love me as I love you."

"How could I know that you . . . felt like . . . that," Safina asked, "or that . . . love could be . . . so miraculous?"

"That is what you are," the Duke said, "and the magic you have brought me, my darling, comes from your heart."

Safina put up her arms to pull down his head to hers.

"Our magic will . . . protect . . . us," she whispered.

"Of course it will, and I promise you," the Duke replied, "that love is stronger than evil."

Safina gave a little sigh of relief.

Then, because the Duke did not want her to think of anything but him, he was kissing her again, kissing her and holding her closer and closer until once more they were moving up towards the stars.

*   *   *

It was difficult the next morning for the Duke to concentrate on the many problems awaiting him downstairs.

They were not able to finish their breakfast before Banks came into the room.

The Overseer wanted a word with them, and the foreman of a group of workmen was waiting for instructions.

Looking at Safina across the table, the Duke thought she had never looked more beautiful.

Her whole face seemed to glow with a new radiance.

When their eyes met, it was impossible for

them to think about anything but the wonder of their love.

"I love you, I love you."

The Duke heard the words repeating themselves in his mind.

He thought he had said them a thousand times during the night.

He was so happy that he knew that if the whole house collapsed, it would not matter as long as Safina was safe.

She must have read his thoughts, because she said:

"It is going to be more beautiful when we have finished than it has ever been, because now we are building, painting, and restoring the love."

"That is just what I was going to say," the Duke exclaimed.

"I knew that was what you were thinking."

"Then is there any point in my telling you that I adore you?"

"I want you to say it," she answered, "I want you to say it a thousand times."

He put out his hand towards her and she saw a sudden sparkle of fire in his eyes.

"Darling, darling, the men are waiting to see you," she murmured.

"Let them wait," the Duke replied as Safina rose from the table.

"We have to do our duty first," she said.

"Now you are bullying me," the Duke complained.

They worked all the morning.

When they had finished a light but delicious luncheon, the Duke said:

"I have something to show you now, at once."

Safina looked at him and asked:

"Is there anything . . . wrong?"

"Not exactly wrong," the Duke replied, "but it cannot wait."

Safina rose and walked towards the door.

"Where is it?" she asked.

"Upstairs," the Duke replied.

They walked up the stairway from which the carpet had already been removed by the workmen.

When they reached the corridor, Safina looked at the Duke for guidance.

Taking her by the hand, he drew her towards his own bedroom.

When he opened the door, she said:

"What has happened? Has something been damaged. Oh, darling, I do hope it is not a piece of the Sèvres china."

"It is more important than that," the Duke said.

She turned around and saw he was locking the door.

Then as he came towards her, she said:

"You do not mean . . . you cannot have . . . brought me . . . here . . ."

"It is important for me to tell you how much I love you," the Duke said, "and quite frankly it cannot wait."

"You made me . . . think it was . . . something

that had . . . gone wrong," Safina said accusingly.

"It would be very wrong if I had to wait any longer to make love to you," the Duke answered.

Her eyes widened and she said:

"But it . . . is only . . . the afternoon . . . I always . . . thought . . ."

The Duke laughed.

"I shall have to teach you, my precious, that any time is the right time for love."

He pulled off his coat as he was speaking and flung it down on a chair.

He put his arms around Safina, and her body melted against his.

It was impossible to think of anything but the wonder of it!

*   *   *

Two hours later the Duke and Duchess came down the stairs.

Safina's cheeks were flushed and her eyes were shining.

The Duke thought that every time he looked at her she was lovelier than ever before.

"I expect there will be a dozen people waiting to see you," she said.

"I am now ready to answer their questions," he replied.

She looked up to smile at him.

As they reached the bottom of the stairs, she saw through the open door a carriage pull up outside.

It was drawn by four horses, and there were two coachmen on the box.

"Visitors!" she exclaimed in a whisper to the Duke.

"I hope not," he answered.

Safina looked again.

Now the carriage door was open and a man was stepping out of it.

She looked at him in astonishment.

Then she gave a cry and ran down the steps towards him.

"Papa!" she exclaimed. "How is it possible that you are here? I thought you were in Scotland."

She flung her arms around the Earl's neck, and he kissed her, saying:

"I drove down from London as soon as I heard where you were."

The Duke, who had followed Safina, held out his hand.

"It is nice to see you, My Lord," he said, "but I am afraid we are in rather a mess."

"I have a great deal to tell you," the Earl replied as they walked up the steps, "so take me where we will not be disturbed."

As he spoke, he looked at the ladders which cluttered the hall and the workmen who were painting the ceiling.

Safina glanced at the Duke.

"I am afraid it must be upstairs, Papa," she said. "All the rooms on the ground floor are being renovated."

The Earl did not answer, but started to climb the staircase.

Looking at him, Safina thought he seemed tired, also, in some strange way, older than ever before.

They walked along the corridor, and she opened the door of her own bedroom.

She remembered guiltily that they had left the bed in the Duke's room without tidying it.

Her own bed had, however, been made by one of the women who had taken up the position of housemaid.

As the room was so large, there was a sofa and two armchairs in front of the fireplace.

The Duke took from the Earl the hat and the cape in which he had travelled.

He put them tidily on a chair against the wall.

Then he asked:

"Can I get you anything to drink, My Lord? But perhaps you have not had luncheon?"

"I had something light to eat on the way," the Earl replied, "and I will have a drink later. I want first to talk to both of you."

There was a note in his voice that made his daughter look at him anxiously.

As he sat down on the sofa, she slipped her hand into his and felt his fingers close over hers almost painfully.

The Duke sat down opposite them, and as her father did not speak, Safina asked:

"Are you . . . angry, Papa, because . . . Crispin and I are . . . married?"

"Not because you are married," the Earl replied, "but at the appalling manner at which it was forced upon you."

"It was ... horrible at ... the time," Safina said, "but now we are very ... very happy. So happy, Papa, that I know it is everything that you have ... wanted for ... me."

The Earl drew in his breath, and then he said:

"Then you are extremely fortunate. I have now to tell you my story because it is something you both have to know."

The pain in his voice was unmistakable.

Safina could only look at him with a worried expression in her eyes and wonder what had occurred.

"As you know," the Earl began, "I left for Scotland a week ago to represent Her Majesty at a very important Meeting which was to take place in Edinburgh."

The Earl paused for a moment before he said:

"You were in Florence and I did not expect you to reach England until after I returned."

Safina parted her lips to explain, but her father went on:

"I naturally had no idea that your Stepmother had contrived that you should come back earlier than I had planned."

"Who told ... you that had ... happened?" Safina asked.

The Earl did not answer.

She guessed he wished to tell the story in his own way, because he continued:

"I arranged to journey to Edinburgh with Lord Burrough, who was also to be a guest of the Duke of Hamilton, and was going by sea in his yacht."

"The most comfortable way to travel," the Duke remarked.

"It should have been," the Earl agreed, "but unfortunately as we emerged from the Thames Estuary into the North Sea there was a sea-fog and we collided with a trawler, or, rather, it collided with us."

Safina gave a cry.

"Papa, you might have been hurt!"

"I was uninjured," the Earl replied, "but Lord Burrough fractured his leg and was also badly bruised."

The Earl paused before he went on:

"There was nothing I could do but bring him back to London, where he could be attended to by his own Physician."

"So you did not get to Scotland," Safina exclaimed.

She realised as she spoke that it was an unnecessary remark.

She was not surprised when her father continued:

"We got back late yesterday evening, and by the time I had escorted Lord Burrough to his house, aroused his servants, got him to bed, and sent for his Physician, it was after midnight."

Safina felt her father's fingers tighten on hers as he said:

"I then went to my own house."

"They did not expect you, Papa?"

"There was no opportunity of informing anyone of my return, nor did I think it was necessary," the Earl replied.

The Duke was watching the Earl as he spoke, and was already anticipating what had happened.

"There is no need for me to go into detail," the Earl went on.

Now his voice was harsh and hard.

There was also an expression in his eyes that made the Duke feel very sorry for him.

"What . . . happened . . . Papa?" Safina said in a bewildered voice.

"I turned your Stepmother and the man who was with her out of my house, and I told her that as I did not want a scandal I would give her five thousand pounds a year as long as she lived abroad."

He paused for a moment and then went on:

"If she ever returned to England, I would immediately institute divorce proceedings against her, citing the man who was with her as co-respondent."

Safina gave a little gasp.

"Do you think she will obey you, My Lord?" the Duke asked.

"I think she will do anything to avoid being ostracized completely by everyone in Society," the Earl replied. "The man I could name as co-respondent has a position at Court and is married with several children."

Safina gasped again.

She knew her Stepmother was wicked, but not so wicked as this.

Then, in a very small voice, she asked:

"What did Stepmama . . . say or do when . . . you turned her . . . out?"

"She cursed me," the Earl replied, "cursed me and you with the vocabulary of a Billingsgate fishwife. I was humiliated and ashamed that I had ever put such a vulgar woman in your mother's place."

As he spoke, Safina looked at the Duke.

She knew that it was her Stepmother's curse that had sent her to him last night.

Then, as she saw the love in his eyes, she knew that however evil the curses might be, they could not touch her now.

She put her cheek against her father's shoulder.

"I . . . am . . . sorry, Papa," she said softly.

"First thing this morning," her father said in a different tone of voice, "I went to the London Office of my Solicitors and was fortunate enough to find Metcalfe himself there."

"So he told you about us?"

"He told me what had happened," the Earl said, "and I knew I must come at once and tell you that it is quite unnecessary for you to raise the loan which Metcalfe told me he had arranged for you."

"But, Papa . . ." Safina began.

"I directed him to transfer to your Account half of your mother's fortune," the Earl continued. "It will amount to nearly a million pounds, which I hope will be enough to restore Wyn."

For a moment there was silence, and then Safina said:

"It is . . . too much, Papa, and . . . you may . . . need more . . . yourself."

"If you are implying," the Earl replied, "that I may marry again, I know now there is 'no fool like an old fool', and I am not so foolish as to make the same mistake twice."

Unexpectedly he smiled.

"If you two are happy, as you have just said you are, then I will concentrate in the future on my grand-children."

Safina blushed and looked shy.

The Duke wanted to put his arms around her and tell her how lovely she was.

Instead, he said:

"That is very generous of you, My Lord, and it is difficult to know how we can thank you."

"There is no reason to thank me," the Earl replied. "It is Safina's money, and I am quite certain that Your Grace will know how to look after it and her."

"I will certainly do my best," the Duke replied, "and I can only say how deeply sorry I am, My Lord, that your life should be so upset."

"I fortunately still have a lot of things to do," the Earl replied, "and I am most interested in seeing what you are doing here."

"Then I have a suggestion to make," the Duke replied.

Safina wondered what it could be.

She realised he was looking at her while speaking to her father.

"As you will understand, My Lord, I would like to take my wife away on a Honeymoon, where we could be alone."

He smiled at Safina before continuing:

"So I am just wondering if in our absence you would supervise, which I think is essential, the restoration we are making to the House and see that the workmen do not waste time."

The Earl stared at him and then he laughed.

"Of course I will!" he said. "Actually there is nothing I would enjoy more."

"Oh, Papa, it sounds wonderful!" Safina cried.

"May I suggest," he continued, "that you start your Honeymoon at my house in Newmarket. Safina has not been there for many years. You will be comfortable there and I think you will both enjoy seeing my Racing-Stables. I will moreover give you half of my horses as a Wedding-Present."

The Duke gasped.

"Do you really mean that?" he enquired.

"I think it is a mistake for your colours to be in abeyance, and it would be amusing to challenge you on a Race-Course."

"It is a wonderful, wonderful idea!" Safina exclaimed. "I cannot tell you how much we both want horses here."

"Then from Newmarket," her father said, "you can go on to Wick Park. The Stables are heavily overstocked, and I suggest that you remove all the horses you require into the Stables here."

Safina jumped up and put her arms around her father's neck and kissed him.

"You are the kindest person in the world," she said.

"You know as well as I do," the Earl replied, "that your mother left me a great fortune, and now I am determined that half of everything I have shall be yours."

He looked at the Duke and said:

"I remember when you were in the Cavalry your Commander-in-Chief telling me what a good rider you were, and I have always thought it sad that since you inherited your title you have not been able to Hunt or take part in the County Steeple-Chases."

"We must make certain that he wins every one of them in the future," Safina said.

"I have got another idea," the Earl remarked.

Safina and the Duke were both listening, and he went on:

"It has always been the ambition of my life to breed the winner of the Derby. As our Estates are near to each other and you are now my son-in-law, why do we not go into partnership? We might even try for the Grand National Steeple-Chase and make it a double!"

For a moment there was silence, and then the Duke said:

"I do not really know what to say. This is so overwhelming that there are no words which will express my feelings, except to say that from the moment Safina became my wife she brought me luck."

"It was the Magic Tree," Safina protested.

"It was—you!" the Duke insisted.

Their eyes met and for a moment they both forgot everything—the horses, the money with which to restore the House, the glory of winning a Classic Race.

There was only one thing that mattered— their love.

A love which came from their hearts and made them not two people but one.

One person enveloped with the Divine Light of real love which comes from God, belongs to God, and is God.

ABOUT THE AUTHOR

Barbara Cartland, the world's most famous romantic novelist, who is also an historian, playwright, lecturer, political speaker and television personality, has now written over 548 books and sold over six hundred million copies all over the world.

She has also had many historical works published and has written four autobiographies as well as the biographies of her mother and that of her brother, Ronald Cartland, who was the first Member of Parliament to be killed in the last war. This book has a preface by Sir Winston Churchill and has just been republished with an introduction by Sir Arthur Bryant.

Love at the Helm, a novel written with the help and inspiration of the late Earl Mountbatten of Burma, Great Uncle of His Royal Highness The Prince of Wales, is being sold for the Mountbatten Memorial Trust.

She has broken the world record for the last sixteen years by writing an average of twenty-three books a year. In the *Guinness Book of Records* she is listed as the world's top-selling author.

Miss Cartland in 1978 sang an Album of Love Songs with the Royal Philharmonic Orchestra.

In private life Barbara Cartland, who is a Dame of the Order of St. John of Jerusalem, Chairman of the St. John Council in Hertfordshire and Deputy President of the St. John Ambulance Brigade, has fought for better conditions and salaries for Midwives and Nurses.

She championed the cause for the Elderly in 1956 invoking a Government Enquiry into the "Housing Conditions of Old People."

In 1962 she had the Law of England changed so that Local Authorities had to provide camps for their own Gypsies. This has meant that since then thousands and thousands of Gypsy children have been able to go to School, which they had never been able to do in the past, as their caravans were moved every twenty-four hours by the Police.

There are now fourteen camps in Hertfordshire and Barbara Cartland has her own Romany Gypsy Camp called Barbaraville by the Gypsies.

Her designs, "Decorating with Love," are being sold all over the U.S.A., and the National Home

Fashions League made her, in 1981, "Woman of Achievement."

She is unique in that she was one and two in the Dalton list of Best Sellers, and one week had four books in the top twenty.

Barbara Cartland's book *Getting Older, Growing Younger* has been published in Great Britain and the U.S.A. and her fifth cookery book, *The Romance of Food*, is now being used by the House of Commons.

In 1984 she received at Kennedy Airport America's Bishop Wright Air Industry Award for her contribution to the development of aviation. In 1931 she and two R.A.F. Officers thought of, and carried, the first aeroplane-towed glider airmail.

During the War she was Chief Lady Welfare Officer in Bedfordshire, looking after 20,000 Service men and women. She thought of having a pool of Wedding Dresses at the War Office so a Service Bride could hire a gown for the day.

She bought 1,000 gowns without coupons for the A.T.S., the W.A.A.F.'s and the W.R.E.N.S. In 1945 Barbara Cartland received the Certificate of Merit from Eastern Command.

In 1964 Barbara Cartland founded the National Association for Health of which she is the President, as a front for all the Health Stores and for any product made as alternative medicine.

This is now a £65 million turnover a year, with one-third going in export.

In January 1988 she received *La Médaille de Vermeil de la Ville de Paris*. This is the highest award to be given in France by the City of Paris. She has sold 25 million books in France.

In March 1988 Barbara Cartland was asked by the Indian Government to open their Health Resort outside Delhi. This is almost the largest Health Resort in the world.

Barbara Cartland was received with great enthusiasm by her fans, who fêted her at a reception in the City, and she received the gift of an embossed plate from the Government.

Barbara Cartland was made a Dame of the Order of the British Empire in the 1991 New Year's Honours List by Her Majesty the Queen for her contribution to Literature and also for her years of work for the community.